YOUNG, HUNG & READY FOR ACTION

YOUNG, HUNG & READY FOR ACTION

Erotic Short Stories

Kenneth Harrison

Leyland Publications
San Francisco

First edition 2001
Front cover photo copyright © 2001 by Kristen Bjorn
Front and back cover design/layout by Stevee Postman

Library of Congress Cataloging-in-Publication Data

Harrison, Kenneth, 1964–
    Young, hung & ready for action : erotic short stories / Kenneth Har-rison.—1st ed.
        155 p. 22 cm.
        ISBN 0-943595-85-1 (alk. paper)
        1. Erotic stories, American.   2. Gay youth—Fiction.   3. Gay men—Fiction.   I. Title: Young, hung, and ready for action.   II. Title.
    PS3558.A67138 Y68   2001
    813'.54—dc21   00-61236
                                                                                        CIP

Leyland Publications
P.O. Box 410690
San Francisco, CA 94141
Complete catalogue of available books is $1 ppd.

CONTENTS

THE COACH'S MEAT 7

HANK'S TRICK 16

KINDRED SPIRITS 25

LOOKING FOR LOVE 33

THE REAL THING 42

THE MEN OF THE HOUSE 52

CONSTRUCTION MEN IN HEAT 63

BILLY'S DAD 72

JAY'S FRIEND 81

MYSTERY MAN 90

BACKSTAGE BLOW BUDDIES 99

GUY TROUBLE 107

FARM BOY FUCKFEST 115

TROUBLE AT MILKWOOD FARMS 123

THE BOYS OF DEL SOL ADVERTISING 132

IT COULD HAPPEN TO YOU 141

PARLOR GAMES 149

THE COACH'S MEAT

Once again Rob and Bobby had finished their weekly after school run with Coach Thompson, and were done showering. Bobby sat on the wood bench set between the two rows of green metal lockers and slipped his long, slender feet into his white crew socks. Except for his socks, Bobby was naked and didn't want to look at Rob for fear of throwing a boner. Behind him, Rob stood with his soft, eight-inch cock dangling between his legs as he towel dried his short blond hair with the orange and white striped towel he'd been using since the beginning of the school year.

Coach Thompson was naked as he strolled past them with a towel draped over his left shoulder. Coach Thompson was tall and rugged, with a crew cut and dark tufts of fur on his upper chest. As always Coach waited until everyone was gone to shower. Between his legs, the coach's shaft dangled. And his hairy balls really dangled pretty low, too. The coach's meat had to be at least nine inches when it was hard, Bobby thought. The coach stepped up to the row of shower heads on the wall, chose the center one, then turned the water on. Bobby's thick slab of cock started to move, so he looked down at the green floor tiles and tried to get his mind off the coach.

Rob gave Bobby a playful shove. "You have to be careful."

Bobby gave Rob the finger, then leaned forward and snagged up his white briefs from the bottom of the locker. Bobby had seen Rob checking guys out before, so who was he to say anything? Bobby slipped his right foot into the leg hole of his briefs, then his left. Standing up, he pulled the briefs up and tucked his meat inside. Already his piss slit had a bead of precum forming on the tip. He rubbed his index finger over the slit, scooped up the drop, then licked it off his finger. Why was he always so damn horny?

"You coming over tonight?" Rob asked as he turned away from Bobby to grab something from his locker.

"Sure will," Bobby said as he checked out the firm curve of Rob's ass, and held himself back from leaning forward and running his tongue along the crack. If it hadn't been for Rob, Bobby would be faced with having to take his senior year of high school over again. Still, he was only a year older than Rob, which wasn't too bad. It would really suck if he was twenty years old and still in high school.

Rob nudged Bobby's shoulder, then pointed to the coach, who had his back facing them as he ran a bar of soap through his ass crack. How great it would be to tickle the coach's pucker with his tongue, Bobby thought, then felt his shaft stiffen. In one fell swoop Bobby reached into his locker and pulled out his oversized Kid Rock t-shirt and pulled it over his head. The bottom of the shirt covered his growing shaft, which made him a little more comfortable. Rob slipped into his boxer shorts, then pulled on his jeans.

"We need to get out of here," Bobby said.

Bobby closed his Algebra book, then turned onto his back. Rob had gone downstairs because his father had wanted him to take out the trash. Bobby ran his toes along the foot board of Rob's bed, touching the thin wooden railings. It was funny how much Rob's room looked like his own, although the rock group posters hanging on Bobby's bedroom walls were of different rock groups than the ones on Rob's walls. Bobby would never think of putting up a Backstreet Boys poster, but Rob had one hung over the head-board. The poster on the wall running along the left hand side of the bed was a poster of The Red Hot Chilly Peppers doing a goof shot of The Beatles' Abbey Road album. It was almost comical that Rob would put up posters of both bands. Grunge versus cute.

It was getting close to summer, and finals were about to begin. Lifting his leg, Bobby scratched his calf. He wished Rob's dad would spring for air conditioning. Even with shorts on Bobby's balls were sweating. Bobby pulled off his t-shirt, then used it to wipe the sweat off his chest. Thanks to Rob he was finally getting the hang of Algebra.

"You would think they could just take the garbage out on their own," Rob said, then closed his bedroom door. He kicked off his sneakers, then flexed the toes of his left foot. His beige shorts hung low on his hips, and his yellow short sleeve button down was open. It didn't look as if he was wearing any underwear.

"I've had it with studying," Bobby said.

"I can tell," Rob said as he pulled his arms out of his shirt and threw it on the floor. He stood in front of Bobby, unfastened his shorts, then let them fall to the floor. Rob's shaft was at half mast, the very tip of the head peeking out from inside the foreskin. Reaching out, Bobby took hold of Rob's fleshy tube and gave it a squeeze. He pulled back on Rob's cock until the hood peeled away from the head, then slipped his lips over the knob and sucked it. Rob placed his hand on the back of Bobby's head and helped him ease his shaft down his hungry throat. "Yes, nice and easy, man," Rob said.

Bobby swallowed the entire eight inches of Rob's prick. He loved the feeling of a cock head plumping up in his throat. Bobby ran his palms along Rob's thighs, then wrapped his fingers around his nut sack just above the two globes resting inside.

"Oh shit, that feels good," Rob whispered as he slowly pulled back.

Bobby gently pulled down on Rob's nuts, then felt his throat fill with cock once more. Taking his free hand, he wrapped his fingers around the base of Rob's shaft and took control of his cock sucking. Keeping his grip near his lips, Bobby quickly pistoned the meaty tube in and out of his mouth. Above him, Rob let out soft moans. Bobby knew hot jizm would soon start spurting. Come on and squirt, Bobby thought and he pulled the meat out of his mouth and tickled the underside of the head with the tip of his tongue. Then Bobby started stroking Rob's cock, watching the hood glide over the purple head with each slip of his fist. He placed his lips over the tip of Rob's dick and continued to stroke.

"Oh shit," Rob groaned, then grabbed a lock of Bobby's hair and pulled his mouth off his cock. "Don't stop. I want to blow my load on your fucking face, man."

Bobby licked his lips as he eagerly continued to stroke Rob's shaft. Finally Rob's knees buckled, then he let out a groan. The first thick blast of hot ball juice shot out of Rob's piss slit and landed on Bobby's lips. The next glob hit the bridge of Bobby's nose and dripped down the right side and onto his cheek. Another shot colored his pink lips with a dollop of cream. The last shot oozed out of the piss slit and over Bobby's fingers. Greedily, Bobby slathered the final remains of Rob's spunk on his face, then took Rob's meat and used it to rub the spuge on into his skin.

"Now it's your turn," Rob said, slapping Bobby's knee. "Take off those shorts."

Bobby pulled his shorts off, then sat down on the bed. As Bobby laid back, Rob grabbed Bobby's ankles, then lifted his legs up over Bobby's head until his toes were almost touching the mattress on either side of his head. Bobby's stiff dick was in front of his face. Sticking out his tongue, Bobby licked the clear drop of precum off the head as he felt Rob's tongue moisten his asshole. Grabbing his fleshy tube, Bobby began to stroke himself.

"Oh man, I want to see you cum," Rob said, then pressed his lips against Bobby's fuck hole and pushed his tongue inside. With quick jabs, Rob tongue fucked Bobby's hole, driving Bobby wild. Placing his tongue against the tip of his cock, Bobby let his jizm shoot. He swallowed every load as it spewed from his slit and landed on his tongue in thick bursts.

When Bobby was finishing blowing his load, Rob let go of his legs and spread out next to him. Closing his eyes, Bobby let his feet dangle off the bed and relaxed. Rob's hand was on his chest, gently rubbing his firm stomach. "You're so fucking hot," Rob whispered.

Bobby turned towards Rob. The scent of his ass was on Rob's breath as he stuck out his tongue and licked Rob's lips. "You know what I would like to do," Bobby said.

"What?" Rob asked.

"Fuck the coach."

Rob grinned, and Bobby knew a plan would soon be underway.

Coach Thompson ran on the outside lane of the track, Rob in the middle lane, and Bobby had the outermost lane. Rob kept his pace with Bobby and the coach as the three of them ran laps around the track, their footfalls making steady repetitive sounds of rubber against tar. None of the three men wore t-shirts, and sweat glistened off their chests and brows in the heat of the mid-day sun. Bobby concentrated on his pacing, and breathing so he wouldn't pop a boner. He and Rob had made their plan, and it was going to happen. At least he hoped it would happen. Finally he would get to suck the coach's cock. Not only that, but Rob would also be there.

"One more lap," Coach Thompson said through heavy breaths.

"Sure, Coach," Rob said. He looked at Bobby and winked. Running along the straight path leading to the first curve, Bobby looked out at the grass and the tennis courts surrounded by a chain link fence a few yards away. It was going to happen, he thought, then cracked a smile. The bend in the track was up ahead. One more lap and the plan would be underway. Bobby fought the urge to sprint through the remainder of the final lap.

Coach Thompson, Rob, and Bobby cut through the gymnasium, then headed towards the entrance to the boys' showers. By the time they were inside, Coach Thompson was still catching his breath, as were Bobby and Rob. It had been a good run, and Bobby was just beginning to feel the workout in his legs. Rob gave Bobby a nudge with his shoulder as the three of them walked into the locker room. Coach Thompson's office door was open on the left.

Pausing at the doorway, Coach Thompson turned towards Bobby and Rob and said, "I'm going to miss running with you boys after you graduate."

"We'll be back for school breaks," Rob said. "We can always put in a few laps then."

"Sounds like a plan," Coach Thompson said, then stepped into his office.

Rob and Bobby walked down the tiled path, past rows of lockers to the right and the open showers to the left. Rob and Bobby both went to their lockers, then peeled off their sweat soaked clothes before eagerly making their way to the showers. Bobby's cock was already half hard, and he hoped it would go down before they went into the coach's office to ask for some soap. Bobby glanced over at Rob and saw that he was in the same condition.

"Shit," Rob said loud enough to be heard in the office. He grabbed his orange and white striped towel, using it to hide the condom he carried, then walked up to the end of the rows of lockers.

Rob waited, then waved Bobby to follow, towel and condom in hand, as he walked towards the coach's office. If Rob's plan didn't work, Bobby hoped the two of them wouldn't get into too much trouble. He didn't know if the coach liked to suck dick, or if he wouldn't mind getting blown by two of his students.

Rob and Bobby walked into Coach Thompson's office to find

the coach stepping out of his jock strap. Standing with his pecker dangling between his legs, Coach Thompson asked what was up.

"I thought I had some soap in my locker, but I don't," Rob said.

"He's a fucking bone head, Coach," Bobby said, trying to act as casual as possible.

Coach Thompson looked Rob and Bobby up and down, then snickered. He opened his metal locker, reached up to the top shelf, took out a green bar of soap, then stepped up to the two boys. "Just don't drop it," he said to Rob, then tossed the bar of soap to him.

Rob caught the soap, then pressed his knuckles against the coach's firm stomach in a fake punch. "Don't you worry about that."

Coach Thompson's cock began to stiffen.

"How come you never shower with us, Coach?" Bobby asked, reaching out and placing his hand on Coach Thompson's upper arm. Bobby met the coach's deep brown eyes, then licked his lips. He slid his hand onto the coach's smooth back. "Are you afraid of us?"

"Not at all," Coach Thompson said.

The soap fell onto the floor, and Rob went down on his knees to pick it up. The coach put his hand on Rob's head, and moved his hardening prick so it was in front of Rob's full lips. Rob wrapped his lips round his meaty shaft and swallowed the entire length in one greedy gulp. Coach's hot breath hit Bobby's face. It was happening, Bobby thought as he ran his fingers through the deep brown hair on the coach's chest.

"Why don't you join him?" Coach said.

Bobby went down on his knees and grabbed the coach's hairy nuts. Rob's head was busy bobbing on the coach's shaft, so Bobby started licking around Coach Thompson's nut sack. Coach parted his legs, and Bobby slipped his hand between them, then pressed his index and middle fingers against his tight pucker until both digits were inside. Bobby felt the coach's ass ring contract. Coach Thompson was tight. Bobby couldn't help but imagine how nice it would feel to have his prick buried deep inside the coach's ass.

Bobby popped the coach's balls out of his mouth, then moved around him. Placing his palms against the coach's firm ass, he parted his cheeks, then dove into his crack. The musty scent of ass filled Bobby's nostrils, driving him wild. Bobby stuck out his tongue and pressed it flat against the coach's pucker, licking the tight hole before tickling it with the tip of his tongue.

Coach Thompson leaned forward, which made it easier for Bobby to get at his fuck hole. He poked his tongue deep inside, then out, slurping and licking away at the tight opening. He stuck his tongue in again and felt the tight ass ring contract. It was going to feel damn good to fuck the coach.

Lips surrounded Bobby's prick. Looking down, Bobby saw Rob lying between Coach's legs as he worked Bobby's cock head. Then Rob grabbed Bobby's nuts and gave them a gentle tug. Bobby leaned away from the coach's ass, then let out a sigh.

Coach Thompson turned around and started slamming his shaft in and out of Bobby's mouth. Spit collected around Bobby's lips, dripping down on his buddy's head. The coach's meat filled Bobby's throat, then was pulled back only to be rammed down again. Coach Thompson held Bobby's head still, then moved his shaft so only the head was in his mouth, then eased his knob back and forth over Bobby's tongue.

"Oh yes, boy, your mouth feels so fucking good," Coach Thompson said.

That was what Bobby wanted. He closed his eyes and eagerly waited for the coach's hot spunk to fill his mouth. Rob was still sucking Bobby's cock head, and it was about to blow.

"Fuck," Coach said through clenched teeth, then pulled his meat out of Bobby's mouth and wrapped his fingers around the hefty shaft. With one stroke hot fuck juice started spurting out of his piss slit and onto Bobby's sweet face. Warm, thick spunk dribbled down Bobby's cheeks, as more of the creamy load splattered against his nose, over his lips and onto his chin. Bobby quickly grabbed the coach's meat as the final squirts dribbled out of the fleshy tube, and rubbed it on his face.

Bobby pulled his meat out of Rob's throat, then stood up. He still had the urge to fuck Coach Thompson's tight ass. "Turn around," he said.

The coach turned around, then placed his hands on his knees. "You want to fuck me, boy?"

"Sure do," Bobby said, snagging a condom from inside his towel, then rolling it onto his shaft. He slid his two middle fingers into Coach Thompson's sweaty ass crack, and rubbed them against his pucker. The coach let out a deep sigh, then pushed his ass even closer to Bobby.

Reaching behind himself, Coach Thompson grabbed hold of Bobby's stiff meat and rubbed against his pucker. "Don't be such a pansy," Coach Thompson said.

Bobby spat on his palm, then used it to grease up the coach's fuck hole before pushing his knob against the tight opening. He pushed, then felt his shaft penetrate. Coach Thompson's ass ring gripped Bobby's shaft as he inched his way inside until his hips were pressed against the coach's butt. Pulling back, Bobby felt his shaft being massaged by heat and moisture. He pushed his cock back in, then out until only the head was inside.

Then Bobby felt Rob's tongue on his asshole, getting it wet with spit, then heard the condom wrapper tear open. Bobby waited for Rob to unroll the latex sheath over his prick before pushing it up his ass, stretching his hole wide to accommodate the girth of Rob's shaft. "Fuck the coach's hole," Rob whispered as he placed his hands on Bobby's hips.

Bobby planted his feet firm on the tiled floor, then held Coach Thompson's hips. With long, fast thrusts, he slammed his fleshy tube in and out of Coach Thompson's hole, at the same time feeling Rob's dick pistoning inside him.

The coach's tight ass ring drove Bobby wild. Already his cock head was filling with jizm, and he felt Rob's swollen knob moving inside his bowels. Rob's hot breath hit the back of his neck in rapid bursts, and Bobby knew his friend was close to losing it.

"Shit, man," Rob called out. Then Bobby felt Rob's knob pulse up his ass as he shot his load inside him.

Bobby planted his root deep inside the coach's fuck chute with one fast thrust, then began to spew his frothy load. He pulled back, then slammed his meat inside once more, shooting more cream.

Bobby felt Rob's tongue flat on his back, then heard him let out a groan. The final remains of Bobby's spunk spilled out of his piss slit as he eased his hips to a stop. Rob pulled his prick out of Bobby's ass, then Bobby pulled his out of Coach Thompson's hole.

Coach Thompson turned towards the two boys as he stroked his prick and blew another creamy load.

"Well boys, I think it's time to hit the showers," Coach Thompson said, once Rob pulled away from his dick.

Bobby playfully slapped Rob's ass. "Let's go," he said, knowing there would be more fun times with the coach.

HANK'S TRICK

The front door slammed shut, and Gary woke with his head pushed into the middle of his Concepts in Economics book. Beyond the book was his pillow, which he pulled closer, then placed under his head. The chrome reading lamp on the night table cast an annoying glow over him, and forced him to keep his eyes shut. If only Hank could be more quiet when he came home, Gary thought. Then he heard Hank hush whoever was with him, then the stairs creaked with each of their footfalls as they made their way upstairs.

Gary reached down and scratched his balls through his white BVDs, feeling his limp prick brush against the soft cotton. The last thing Gary needed was to spend the night listening to Hank fuck some guy up the ass. Gary turned off the reading lamp.

Now Hank and his buddy were creeping past Gary's bedroom door. It was finals week and Hank had been getting laid non stop. Gary knew Hank was smart, but didn't he ever have to study?

Gary closed the Economics book, then dangled it over the edge of the bed and let it go. The book fell with a dull thud as Hank's bedroom door closed. There was the sound of buckles, and shoes being dropped. An occasional Shh. Then Hank's voice, "Shit, man, suck it."

Hank had said that to Gary a few times when they'd first met, which made the goings on in Hank's bedroom more vivid. At seven inches in circumference, Hank's cock had been the thickest he'd seen. Gary had had a hard time getting his throat relaxed enough to swallow the entire length of eight inches.

Hank's voice came through the wall again, "You can do it, man. Come on."

Gary wondered if Hank used the same lines on everyone. Hank had placed his hand on the back of Gary's head as Gary had grabbed the thick fleshy tube, his fingers barely meeting. A thin vein wound its way along the left side of Hank's dick, and the head was perfectly formed.

"Oh, that's great, man. That's great," Hank said. "Suck it all."

Gary assumed the guy with Hank was having a good time. He wondered if the man sucking Hank's dick was another student, or just some guy he'd picked up at a bar or rest area. Gary had met Hank in Western Civilizations class, which both were taking as a prerequisite. After the first week of the class, Hank had asked Gary if he'd want to study with him. After noticing the massive bulge running down Hank's left leg, Gary had accepted the invitation. And that was when Gary had learned that Hank could read anything and know it cold, so history was a subject he enjoyed. Hank had aced the class, while Gary had received a B-plus.

There was the sound of cock slapping against skin coming from Hank's bedroom. Hank loved slapping his cock against guys' faces. Remembering how Hank had done that to him, Gary's shaft became stiff. Reaching into his BVDs, past the bush of dark brown pubic hair, Gary grabbed his prick and gave it a stroke. Although Gary's cock was nowhere close to meeting Hank's dimensions, it had a solid feel. It was five inches in circumference, and a good six inches in length. Smooth and uncut. He liked the way the foreskin slid over the head when he stroked up, then slid back on the down stroke.

"Relax and take it, man," Hank said in the next room.

When Gary had been on his hands and knees, Hank had pushed his meat into his asshole. Gary's ass ring had stretched wide to accommodate Hank's shaft, and every inch had been a challenge as it eased inside him. And when Hank had been inside, he'd reached around Gary's waist, grabbed hold of Gary's rod and stroked it.

The bed in Hank's room started hitting the wall in steady intervals. Hank was really giving it to the guy. Gary pulled off his briefs, parted his legs, then started playing with his tight little fuck hole. He pressed his middle and index fingers against his pucker, feeling the ring give way and grip the tips.

"Your ass feels good," Hank said.

Gary brought his fingers up to his mouth, the sweet scent of his ass filling his nostrils, tantalizing him. He stuck his fingers in his mouth, then eased them down his throat. Hank's bed continued to slam against the wall. Gary stroked his prick as he sucked his fingers. Hot ball juice started filling his shaft, building up at the head.

"Shit, man, I'm going to cum," Hank said.

Gary's legs tightened, his back arched. Cum on my face, Gary thought, pulling his fingers out of his mouth and wiping them on his cheeks. Cum all over my face. Then his cock head pulsed, and the first shot of spunk burst out of his piss slit and hit his chest, then another and another. His body buckled with each shot, until his nuts were empty.

The pounding of Hank's bed against the wall slowed, and soft moans seeped through the walls. Gary closed his eyes and fell asleep.

Ed stood in front of the beige Formica counter top and poured coffee into his big purple mug. Wearing only a terry cloth velcro wrap around, his smooth, well sculpted body was in plain view. Add to that Ed's military issue haircut, and he looked more like a Marine than a physics major. And Gary knew that was why men threw themselves at him any chance they got.

Gary's morning hardon pressed out against his white BVDs as he reached over the counter, grabbed a mug from the cupboard, then poured himself a cup of coffee.

"Did you hear them last night?" Ed asked.

"They woke me up," Gary said. "I think it's time we had a little talk with him about this. It's getting out of hand."

Ed brought the purple mug of steaming coffee to his lips, took a sip, then put the mug down on the counter. "I don't know about you, but I would like to find out who he's been fucking."

"Do you think it's the same guy?" Gary asked.

"I've noticed that it takes less and less time for Hank to get his cock up the guy's ass, and you know how big Hank is. Getting Hank's prick up any ass takes quite some time." Ed crossed his arms. "But then again, I've always been tight."

"The topic of the morning is Ed's ass, I see," Hank said, standing in the doorway, his big prick bobbing beneath a pair of gray sweat pants. He rubbed his fingers through the dark hair on his chest. "Is there any more coffee?"

"Help yourself," Ed said, stepping away from the counter. "Actually, we were wondering who you've been fucking."

"Have you ever heard of discretion?" Hank said.

Ed turned towards Gary. "Three gay men under one roof, and he wants to be discreet. Have you ever heard of such a thing?"

"Sometimes it's needed," Hank said before Gary could get a word in. "Not everyone is out of the closet, despite what the two of you might think."

"A boyfriend," Ed said playfully. "I didn't think you believed in such things. What about your independence?"

Hank grinned, grabbed his coffee mug, then walked out of the kitchen.

Ed turned towards Gary, a fiendish grin forming. Gary knew trouble was coming.

Gary couldn't believe he was hiding in Hank's closet, waiting for him to get home. Ed had talked him into finding out who Hank had been secretly fucking, and had made Gary curious about it, too. If they got caught, Hank would be pissed, and for good reason. It's not that Gary didn't want to know who the guy taking Hank's cock was, but hiding in Hank's closet was a bit extreme. Although Ed had made it all sound much more fun when he'd convinced Gary to join him in his quest. It hadn't been until Gary had actually stepped into Hank's closet, closed the double doors and made sure both he and Ed were positioned in front of the slatted panels set into the doors that he had felt awkward about their plan. Thankfully Ed was standing next to him, arms close to his side, a pair of white button down shirts separating them.

Ed sighed.

"Quiet," Gary said. He didn't need Ed sighing and not realizing it once Hank was home with his trick.

Ed placed his hand on Gary's back, right above his ass. "Sorry."

The front door to the house opened, then slammed shut. Gary's cock began to stir with excitement as he held his breath. Ed shifted, and the clothes began to sway. Two sets of footfalls landed on the steps in steady intervals. Gary bit his lower lip and waited. Gary's palms were sweating, so he wiped them against his jeans. The back of Ed's hand brushed past Gary's. Hank and his trick were in the hall, walking towards Hank's bedroom door. The door opened with a creak, then the light went on, making it easy for Gary to see through the slats set in the door. Hank's partner was too far to the left for Gary to see him. Ed was also peering in the direction of Hank's guest.

Hank pulled off his t-shirt, then kicked off his sneakers. Next came Hank's jeans, and his big tube of flesh fell out of his pants and bobbed at half mast. Hank gave his prick a stroke. "You like it?" he asked.

"I sure do," the man said, his voice deep and familiar. A blue striped Oxford shirt was thrown into view by Hank's partner. Then the partner's hairy leg came into view, then the rest of his torso, which was tall and lean, with a smooth, defined chest and thin waist. The trick's cock was stiff, rising up five inches, then bending to the left. Gary bent his knees, then saw the man's downward sloping nose, his soft brown hair, his olive complexion. Then it hit him. Hank was fucking that new guy who was teaching Contemporary Literature: Professor Jensen.

Ed tapped Gary's hand, then looked wide eyed. He mouthed, Professor Jensen. Gary nodded, then Ed mouthed, Hot. It was hot, but Gary didn't know why Hank had decided to fuck Professor Jensen.

The professor was on his knees, his mouth open and taking in every last inch of Hank's shaft. And Hank had his hand on top of the professor's head, his fingers buried in the soft brown strands of his hair.

Ed's hand fell to Gary's crotch, and squeezed his meaty bulge. Spreading his legs, Gary reached over to Ed's crotch, his hand meeting up with Ed's cock and balls, which were already hanging out of his jeans. Gripping Ed's firm shaft, Gary started stroking it. If there was more room, he'd go down on Ed. But he couldn't.

Ed fumbled with the buttons of Gary's jeans, and, after a minute was able to get them all undone. Ed pulled Gary's stiff meat out of the fly. Now things were getting interesting, Gary thought. Peeking through the slats in the door, Gary watched as the professor sucked Hank's big balls into his mouth.

"That feels real good, man," Hank said, slapping his shaft against the professor's face. "My cock is going to feel real good up your ass, too."

Ed's grip was tight around Gary's prick, slowly stroking it, making the foreskin glide over the ripe head. Gary stroked Ed with the same ease, keeping it nice and slow so neither of them would shoot his load too quick.

"Get up and bend over," Hank said.

The professor stood, bent, then reached around and spread his ass cheeks. Hank spit on his fingers, then stuck them up the professor's butt. Professor Jensen shook his ass as Hank gave his hole a good finger fuck. Then the professor turned, and the two men kissed.

Ed squeezed Gary's shaft, then grinned. Gary was also excited, but he didn't want to get himself worked up too much. Ed shifted, then lost balance and fell into the door.

"What was that?" Hank asked, looking at the closet. Gary held his breath. Hank was going to find them behind the door. The handle to the closet jiggled, then both doors flew open. And there was Hank, naked, his hardon rising up between his legs. "What the fuck are you two doing here?" Hank asked, then looked down at Gary's boner. "You fucking pigs were jerking off while watching me fuck."

"We were curious about who you were fucking," Ed said.

Hank turned towards Professor Jensen. "Well, Jeff, these are my roommates."

"I'm really sorry about this," Gary said. "We were just curious."

"And it got the best of you guys," Hank said, reaching out and grabbing hold of Gary's softening prick and giving it a squeeze. "I bet you two just wanted to have a little fun."

"Yes, we did," Ed said. "We'll make it up to you somehow."

"That you will." Hank grabbed his shaft and waved it at Gary and Ed. "I think you boys ought to start making up for it now."

Gary stepped out of the closet, then Ed followed. Hank's dick looked inviting, big and thick and hard. Hank gave it another shake as Professor Jensen sat on the edge of the bed. Gary had watched the professor suck Hank's cock, so why not the other way around? And it wasn't as if Gary didn't want to suck Hank's meat. Gary's stiff dick attested to that.

Going down on his knees, Gary gripped Hank's prick, feeling the weight of his shaft. Hank placed his hand on the back of Gary's head. "That's right, suck it," Hank said.

Gary opened his mouth and slipped the bulbous cock head inside, then ran his tongue around the swollen knob. He slowly slipped the rest of the shaft down his throat. Hank's big, hairy balls hit Gary's chin in steady intervals as Hank slid his prick back and forth. The ripe cock head swelled in Gary's throat, pushing out against the inside of his stretched gullet, getting ready to spew its frothy contents.

Then Ed was naked, down on his knees next to Gary. Hank slid his hips back, easing his shaft out of Gary's mouth. Drool spilled from Gary's lower lip and puddled on the floor, then Hank's dick was held in front of Ed's open lips.

Gary undressed and watched Ed swallow Hank's shaft in one gulp. And behind Hank was the professor, kneeling down, his face buried in Hank's ass.

Hank motioned for Gary, and Gary stood next to him as Hank wrapped his big hand around his waist, feeling his smooth ass. Hank dipped his fingers between Gary's ass cheeks. He pushed two fingers against Gary's pucker, then slipped both tips inside. The two men kissed long and deep. When their lips parted, Hank said, "I'm going to fuck you up the ass."

Gary looked down, watching Hank fuck Ed's beautiful mouth, his lips glossed with spit. It had been a while since Gary had been fucked, and having that huge slab of meat sliding up his hole wasn't going to be easy.

"I have some condoms on top of the bureau," Hank said.

Gary walked over to the bureau, grabbed a condom and the tube of lubricant, then handed them to Hank. Hank opened the wrapper, then unrolled the condom over his shaft. Then Gary turned, put his hands on his knees and waited for Hank to slather his fuck hole with lube.

"This is going to feel good," Hank said, slapping his shaft against Gary's tight pucker. He pressed the head against the hole, then pushed inside, stretching Gary's hole open to accommodate the head. Hank paused, then slipped another inch inside.

Gary closed his eyes, breathed in deep and steady. It had been a long time since he'd last been fucked, and having Hank's thick prick up his ass wasn't going to be easy. Gary's sphincter stretched wider as more of Hank's meat slipped inside. Hank paused, then, with one quick thrust, he pushed the remainder of his shaft inside Gary's fuck canal. Pain shot through Gary's gut, and he hoped Hank wouldn't go to town and start fucking him uncontrollably.

"You okay, man?" Hank asked, keeping his shaft buried inside Gary's body.

"Sure, I'm fine," Gary said. Sweat had beaded up on Gary's brow and upper lip, and he took a few deep breaths.

Hank gently rubbed Gary's back. "Just relax and get used to being full of my meat."

Professor Jensen stood in front of Gary, and wrapped his hand around the back of his neck. The professor's prick stood erect in front of Gary's face, a pearl of precum sparkling on the piss slit. Opening his mouth, Gary took the professor's shaft.

"That's right," Hank said, "suck his cock."

After swallowing Hank's shaft, the professor's dick went down smooth. Gary swallowed and sucked the fleshy shaft as it was rammed in and out of his mouth, the head coming close to the edge of his lips, then plunging back down his throat.

Hank's cock started working Gary's ass, pistoning in and out of his fuck hole in time with Professor Jensen's prick. Ed crouched down beneath Gary and placed Gary's stiff dick in his mouth. Gary closed his eyes and tried desperately not to blow his load. But Ed's sucking mouth, the smoothness of his tongue against the bottom of his shaft, and the way his lips brushed against the head made it difficult to hold back. Already his cock head was feeling the pressure of cum wanting to shoot. And the bulbous knob in his mouth seemed about ready to pop, too.

Then Hank let out a grunt, thrust his shaft deep inside Gary's ass, and his cock head began to pulse. "Oh fuck, man," Hank called out, tightening his grip on Gary's waist as he unloaded his hot spunk.

As the last drops of Hank's cum shot out, Gary couldn't hold his load back. Gary pulled the professor's shaft out of his mouth, stood slightly and grabbed his own shaft. Ed leaned back as Gary stroked himself to a creamy froth. His first shot hit Ed square on the chest, then his second landed just under Ed's pectorals. The rest covered Ed's stomach and dripped down into his pubic hair.

Hank's prick slid out of Gary's ass. Both Gary and Hank watched Ed and the professor stroke their meat. Ed was on the floor, and the professor stood over him. Then the professor's legs tightened, and he shot his load on Ed's chest and stomach. Each thick glob of hot jizm splattered against Ed's flesh, and some of the thick spunk mixed with Gary's load.

Ed continued to stroke his shaft, then he let out a grunt and added his load to the mess that coated his body.

Looking up at the three men, Ed grinned. "Anyone have a towel?" he asked.

"Why don't you just go and take a shower?" Hank said, then

turned towards Gary. "Mind if we actually get some privacy now?"
"Sure," Gary said, then gathered his clothes and left. Hopefully
Hank wouldn't decide to move. He had enjoyed himself all the
same, and it seemed as if Hank had, too. As for Professor Jensen,
that was another story. Hank wasn't taking any literature classes,
so it wasn't as if he was fucking the guy for a good grade. Was he
doing it just because he thought the guy was hot? And why would
a college professor risk being caught fucking a student just for a
fuck? Gary was puzzled. Were they lovers? The thought seemed
absurd, especially since Hank had too often said that he'd never
want to give up his independence.

Gary listened to Hank and the professor walk down the hall.
This time there was only one set of footsteps heading down to the
first floor. Gary's bedroom door opened, and in walked Hank
wearing only his BVDs. Arms crossed, he stood in front of Gary.
"Jeff is worried that you and Ed will tell people about us," Hank
said. "He's new here, and a professor. It wouldn't look good for
him if it got out that he was having an affair with one of the
students."

"An affair?" Gary said. "You two are boyfriends?"

Hank nodded. "I like him . . . a lot."

"I won't tell anyone," Gary said.

"I hope not," Hank said. "Let me go talk to Ed."

"I am sorry about this," Gary said. "We just got caught up in
the moment is all."

"Give me some time, I'll get over it," Hank said. "The weird
thing is that Jeff thought it was kind of hot."

"And if he didn't?" Gary asked.

"Then I'd be a lot more pissed off than I am now. In a way you
guys are pretty lucky you both know how to fuck. Between you
and me, Jeff wants to do it again." Hank winked, then stepped out
of Gary's bedroom.

Gary listened as the bathroom door was opened, and the sound
of the shower was clearer than before. Then the door closed, and
the sound of the shower was muffled again. Gary wondered how
Ed would take the news of Hank actually having a boyfriend. Not
only that, but Ed had been right that day in the kitchen.

"Holy shit!" Ed called out, his voice echoing down the hall.

Gary hoped Ed could keep a secret.

KINDRED SPIRITS

It wasn't until my senior year of Stanton Trials High School, at the age of eighteen, that my buddy, Jared, started sprouting dark hair on his chest. That was when I really started to notice him. It's not that Jared had never had a nice body before then, he'd always kept in shape, but he'd suddenly become more masculine. And I, being smooth, was in awe of his body. Every chance I had to see his big hairy nuts, or his thick seven-inch cock, I took. And I had had plenty of opportunity to view his body. It wasn't that we had gym class together, because we didn't, it's just that we were buddies. Not to mention that we'd carved out our own spot in the overgrown brush down by Seymore Lake.

Aside from shucking off our clothes and skinny dipping in the lake, we used to study for exams there, too. I loved how the water clung to the hair on Jared's body, and how he'd quickly glide his hand down his legs and chest to slice off the excess moisture. And watching him do just that gave me more than a few sexual fantasies, not to mention the wet dreams I'd started having of him.

We'd both been accepted to Boston College on early enrollment, and were excited about getting out of our little hick town. We'd been studying for finals down at our secret hideaway by the lake, and I just couldn't cram another thing into my brain. Feeling the hot sun on my body, and having nice cool water just inches away from our open books, I yanked off my shirt, then started on my shorts. "I can't shove another thing into this skull!" I said.

That was all Jared needed to hear to slam his book closed and pull off his shirt. I got a good peek at Jared's bare chest, thick cock and hairy nuts. It seemed that Jared didn't much mind my looking, the way he strutted past me shaking his hairy ass, then stopped at the edge of the lake. With my body lacking so much hair, I felt like a little boy next to him.

"What are you waiting for?" Jared asked, giving my bare ass a pat. Then Jared ran into the water, his big dick flopping around half-hard and heavy, making me think it was going to bruise his thighs and stomach. Even in cold water, when your privates do some shrinking and look small, his shaft still looked larger than life. It was hard not to look at it, and sometimes he'd catch me staring and say that if I wanted to look at it so bad I should just go ahead and take a picture. But that day, the day we went swimming, I did real good about not looking at it for too long. The both of us just floated around on top of the water, arms outstretched, looking up at the sky. Then Jared said, "You know, when my dad was eighteen he could drink."

"They must have changed the laws," I said, knowing Jared had something cooking. I dove underwater and snuck a peek at Jared's firm hairy ass, then came back up to the surface. I admired the way Jared's body looked riding on top of the water the way it did, his cock and balls just flopped over on his thigh. Water clung to the hair on his chest and sparkled in the sun.

"How about you meeting me here tonight after supper?" Jared said. "Just come on by and I'll be here waiting for you."

I let my feet sink and started treading water. But Jared kept on floating. "What are you thinking?" I asked.

"It's Saturday night, come on, let's have some fun."

When Jared had a thought in his head, he didn't let it go. And, not wanting to argue, I just said, "Sure, why not." I snuck another glance at Jared's dick, then at the thick patch of hair on his chest. It was hard not to wonder how good it must feel to have a body like his, so masculine. The body of a man.

Small clouds of dirt rose at my feet with each step, and the tire treads of our next door neighbor's truck were still fresh in the dirt as I trod along the path leading home with my hands stuffed in my pockets to hide my boner. It wasn't that anyone ever wandered down the road where I lived with my dad, but more that I was afraid someone just might decide to take that path and see me sporting a woody. Both our house and our neighbor's, Mr. Price, were kind of close to each other. Mr. Price had this small red four-square house, with a porch out front and a rocking chair that he'd sometimes use late at night while drinking a beer and doing some reading. Practically every inch of his burly frame had hair on it, and my dad sometimes called him the bear instead of Al, which was his first name.

When I got home from the lake, Mr. Price was out in his front yard mowing the last of his lawn. He didn't have a shirt on. Mr. Price reached the edge of his lawn, then turned the mower around and spotted me approaching. "Are you checking out my lawn, boy?" Mr. Price asked, then turned the lawn mower off.

"It looks good, Mr. Price," I said.

"You go tell that to your father. He's been at me all week about it." Mr. Price was joking around about my dad riding him about his lawn, he and my daddy were good friends.

"I'll do that," I said.

"And tell him that you're welcome to drop by tonight, if you want. We're going to watch a movie and eat some popcorn."

"I'm going to Jared's tonight, but thanks all the same," I said. "What are you watching?"

"Mildred Pierce. It's a murder mystery starring Joan Crawford."

"Maybe next time," I said, then headed home.

After dinner, I cleared the plates and did the dishes with my dad. We'd had leftover lasagna that my father had made earlier that week and saved for a day when he didn't have time after work at the garage to make a decent meal. He'd started making meals that would feed us for two or three days when I was five and mom had walked out on us. I washed and he dried, then put the dishes away in the old nineteen fifties style cupboards he'd always wanted to replace but never did.

Before I left to meet up with Jared, my dad was about to hop into the shower. With my father wrapped in a thick, green towel, the bulge of his cock and balls swaying beneath the towel as he walked, I noticed how similar our bodies were. Although he was older, his body was smooth, lean and tight. I knew that if I turned out like my dad, my chest would remain hairless.

"Don't stay out too late," my father said before stepping into the bathroom.

Jared wasn't at the lake by the time I got there. It being a warm night and all, I took off my socks and sneakers, then rubbed my feet in the grass. Crickets chirped, and a few fireflies glowed in the distance. The moon lit a bright yellow streak on top of the lake. I let out a sigh, then took a seat. It wasn't long before I heard some rustling out in the brush, then saw Jared's head poke out at me.

"I failed," Jared said. "No beer."

"That's okay." I looked up at the night sky. "It's real nice out anyhow."

"You still want to hang out?"

I didn't see why not. Getting drunk wasn't high on my priorities, so I told him it was okay. Jared sat down and gave me a friendly punch on the arm. "How about we go for a dip? It's nice enough."

Being naked with Jared was better than anything else I could think of, so I said yes and we peeled off our clothes and dove in. Jared was kind of playful, swimming under my legs, then coming up to give me a surprise dunk. We swam around some, and when we were exhausted, we got out of the water and spread out on the grass. We stared up at the moon for a while, catching our breath, and I fought the urge to reach out and put my arm on Jared's chest and push my fingers through the thick patch of hair on his chest. As it was my dick had already started growing hard. I knew it was going to be difficult not to think about doing things with Jared. I turned to look at him, and our eyes met.

"You think you'll ever sprout chest hair?" Jared asked.

I turned to my side and propped my head up with my hand. "Is your dad hairy?" I asked even though I knew he was.

"That he is," Jared said.

"I doubt it, then." I pulled on some blades of grass, then glanced over at Jared's body. "Does it get scratchy having all that hair?"

"You'd think it would, but it doesn't," Jared said, running his fingers through his damp fur. "Feel it."

That was all it took for me to reach out and push my fingers through the thick patch. Hairs curled over my fingers, and I felt the heat from his body underneath. My dick was already hard, and precum began to form on the tip.

Jared turned to me and smiled. He reached out and touched my chest with his cold hand, but I didn't move. Instead I slid my fingers through his hair, down towards his stomach and the thin line of fur leading towards his pubic bush.

Jared's hot breath hit my face, then I felt his lips pressed against mine; his hand slid around my waist. He pulled me close, so close I felt his coarse chest hair against my body. We kissed long and deep. Then our lips parted, and Jared kissed my neck and his hands slid over my ass. He dipped his fingers into the crack, sliding his middle finger between my legs as they separated.

Jared rolled me onto my back, and looked down at me. Without saying a word, we just looked at each other. I placed my hands on his hairy ass, then slipped my fingers down to the crease where his buns met his legs. My cock was pressed against his body, and I felt his warmth as I'm sure he felt mine. I parted his ass cheeks and felt his tight hole with my middle finger.

"Wet it and stick it in," Jared said.

I brought my fingers up to my mouth and inhaled the sweet smell of Jared's ass, then stuck both middle and index fingers in my mouth and sucked on them before putting them back in his crack. Jared rubbed his stiff dick against my stomach and let out a sigh as my finger slid into his tight butt.

Jared leaned forward, nibbled on my right earlobe, then ran his tongue along the edge of my ear. "I want you to suck my cock," he said.

I took my fingers out of his ass, then Jared moved up so his hairy nuts were on my lips. I reached up and grabbed hold of his prick, feeling the massive girth of his shaft for the first time. The enormity of it amazed me, even after having seen it so many times. Precum seeped out of the piss slit, running down the thick tube of flesh. Jared pushed his shaft down so the head was against my lips, then pushed it into my mouth. I greedily sucked the head, feeling it fill my mouth. Then Jared started moving his hips so his shaft slid back and forth on my tongue.

"That feels good," Jared said. Then he slipped his prick out of my mouth and sat on the grass. He moved so his crotch was near my mouth and mine was next to his. Then he took my fleshy tube between his lips and started sucking on it. He swallowed the entire length in one gulp, then bobbed his head on it.

I grabbed Jared's nuts, sucked them into my mouth, then let them pop out. Jared opened his legs, and I saw his tight fuck hole wink at me. Leaning in, I slid the flat of my tongue against his pucker and started licking away. I couldn't get enough of Jared's sweet hole. I stuck my tongue deep inside, then licked around the creased opening.

Jared let out soft, muffled moans of pleasure as he continued to suck on my prick. I was close to shooting my load, but wanted to make it last. This was my first sexual experience, and I knew it was also Jared's. If he'd had sex before this he would have told me. Jared's fingers gripped the base of my cock, then his mouth worked the plump head. I felt my load building up at the head, eager to burst. I let out a groan. "No, not yet," I said through clenched teeth. But Jared wouldn't let up. He sucked my cock down to the root again, then slid it out of his throat until the head was back on his lips.

I grabbed Jared's dick and rammed it down my throat. I sucked his cock with the same fury that Jared did mine. Then it was too late. My legs tightened, and I knew my load was about to blow. I swallowed Jared's rod, then felt my cock head pulse and spew hot spunk into my friend's mouth. He swallowed every shot, then let his own jizm spew on my tongue. It seemed as if Jared's sweet load would never stop, but it did, and I swallowed every last drop of it.

When Jared and I had finished coming, Jared moved by my side on the grass and wrapped his arm around me. I could smell my spunk on his breath, and the aftertaste of his creamy load was in my mouth. I kissed Jared's chest, then reached up and gently ran my tongue over his lips. In the background, crickets chirped and I felt so happy being there with Jared. But I knew it wouldn't last, that we'd both have to go home.

"We should keep this to ourselves," Jared said.

I couldn't believe what I was hearing. I didn't want to treat what had just happened between us like some dirty secret, and didn't know what to say, so just stared up at the night sky.

"Did you hear me?" Jared said.

"Yes, I heard you," I said. I hated him for saying what he'd said, but kind of understood that some people wouldn't understand what had just taken place between us. "I'm not ashamed." I said. "We didn't do anything wrong."

"Neither am I," he said.

"Then why are you acting like some dumb hick?"

Jared wrapped his big strong arm around my shoulders, then kissed my forehead. His chest hairs tickled my nose, so I pursed my lips and blew on them. "I'm not a dumb hick," he said. "I just know people, and they won't treat us right."

I was silent for the rest of the time we were there. Jared periodically asked if I was okay, and I said that I was although it was a lie. Deep down there was a part of me that wanted to punch Jared in the face and scream at him. I had waited too long to show him how I felt, and now that I had he'd started acting as if it had been shameful.

Walking home, all I could think about was not being able to tell anyone about what I'd done with Jared. I kept telling myself that it didn't matter, that I didn't have to explain my feelings to anyone; that I wasn't trying to prove anything. But it did matter. I wanted to tell someone, my father, anyone. I felt isolated.

As I approached my home, I noticed a flickering light in Mr. Price's living room windows. I figured Mr. Price and my dad must have started the movie late. I was curious about the movie, and at the same time didn't want to bother them, so I decided to peek in the window instead of knocking on the door. Standing in the bushes outside Mr. Price's house, I peered inside. Mr. Price and my father were completely naked. Mr. Price's cock looked to be a good six thick inches. My father was on his knees in front of Mr. Price, stroking his own meaty shaft. I watched my dad take Mr. Price's cock in his mouth and swallow the entire length down his throat. Mr. Price grabbed my dad's head and moved his hips so his shaft slid in and out of my father's mouth.

Moving to the side, I ducked some and kept peeking in at them. It was amazing to see my father suck our neighbor's dick, not to mention how he'd later leaned back and grabbed a condom and unrolled it over Mr. Price's shaft. Lying on his back with his legs in the air, my dad allowed Mr. Price to shove his cock up his ass. Mr. Price's shaft slid into my dad's butt with no trouble at all. My father wrapped his legs around Mr. Price's lower torso as he got fucked with long hard jabs.

I moved back into the darkness, just far enough that I could still watch the two men doing something like what I'd done with Jared. I watched as my dad started playing with his own shaft, giving long slow strokes. Then Mr. Price reached out and started to twist my father's nipples as he continued to slip his prick in and out of my dad's ass. And that was when my father's legs jerked up, and he shot his creamy load.

I stepped away from the window before they saw me watching. It was amazing to see my father having sex with another man, and made me wonder how long the two of them had kept it a secret. Why hadn't my father ever told me about him and Mr. Price? Had he thought I wouldn't have understood? It was an odd, comforting feeling unlike anything I'd felt before. Somehow I'd have to find a way to tell my dad about me and Jared, but had no idea how I would do it. All I knew was that I had to, that things had to come out in the open.

I let things go on the way they were until I'd moved to college with Jared. I shared a room with Jared, and we'd moved the twin beds together. I told my dad about the beds, then asked if Mr. Price ever slept over. My dad said he did, and that he was happy for me.

LOOKING FOR LOVE

Steve always said you can do anything as long as you act as if you're allowed, then expected me to act like I'd never heard that one before. The thing was, I also knew that there's a difference between knowing something and believing it. Steve believes it, but he can. Steve's my roommate, and long time friend. He's handsome, with dark skin and eyes, dark wavy hair, a chiseled jaw line and a smooth body that's slender, yet defined. And if that isn't enough, Steve can wear any kind of jeans without a cock ring and look like he's packing the biggest basket you've seen in a long time, simply because he is.

There's nothing outstanding about me. I'm neither handsome nor ugly. My body isn't built, but it's not flabby either. As far as my dick goes, it's only six inches, somewhat thick, but not excessively. Steve thinks I have big balls, and I've had other guys say the same, so it must be true. They're hairy, though. I refuse to shave them. Take me as I am, you know. What I'm trying to say is that I've never been the kind of guy who can get away with anything. No ifs, ands, or buts. And that's what makes this interesting.

I met Steve during my junior year of college, just after finals. We met at this downtown club called Mirabar. The middle of the second floor of Mirabar was cut out, and a metal railing surrounded the opening, which overlooked the dance floor. The first time I saw Steve, he was on the second floor, leaning over the railing and peering down at the boys on the dance floor below. Behind him, men staggered about in the dark, smoky club talking to friends, and searching for that night's boy toy. But Steve kept his gaze down, occasionally taking a swig of beer from the bottle dangling between his fingers, then looking back. Due to his stunning looks, I pegged Steve for one of the untouchables. However, that didn't stop me from sidling up next to him and watching the crowded dance floor.

Steve said hello first, which surprised me. I didn't think guys like Steve ever made the first move. I tried to stay cool, grinning and nodding hello. "Looking for love?" I asked, hoping I didn't sound dumb.

Steven turned towards me, his eyes sparkling through the dim light and smoke. "Anything but," he said. "How about you?"

Well, I wasn't looking for love, but wasn't about to shoo it away if it decided to land on my lap. But I knew that admitting that would be an easy death with Steve, so I said that I was looking for fun, which seemed to put him at ease. Fun was something he understood, and after we finished our drinks, we were off to Steve's place.

Steve's roommate was sleeping over at his new boyfriend's, so we had the apartment all to ourselves. Steve lived on the East Side of Providence, in a small two bedroom apartment with a hodge podge of used furniture that didn't match. Once inside, we started kissing, and his hands went straight to my ass as his boner pressed against my thigh. I don't want to get into blow by blow detail, but let me say, Steve knows how to eat ass. He slurped up my hole like it's never been licked before. He also fingered my ass, and sucked my balls like a pro. Let me tell you, the guy was made for sex. And I was in my glory, too. I mean, here was this handsome man, with the kind of cock that makes you hold your breath before it plunges down your throat. And his shaft felt real good gliding over my tongue while he fucked my mouth.

When Steve comes, every muscle in his body gets tight, his toes curl and he lets out this beautiful groan. Then he starts spurting thick buckets of jizm that shoot out like water from a plastic water pistol. And that first night, the way his ball juice splattered against my chest almost made me cream, too. After four or so shots he usually peters out, though.

After that, Steve and I became pretty good friends. We went out together, played around together, even studied together. And we had our share of hot three-ways. If there was one thing I learned about Steve, it was that he loved hot sex. And he would do anything to get it, he had no fear. And, being with him made you feel as if you, too, were hot and desirable. I know it sounds stupid, but that's how it made me feel, being around him. Steve always said it was because he gave me a little more confidence, and that it had nothing to do with him. I never believed him, though. And how could I, he was so damn beautiful. He could do anything.

One summer, while we were heading home from P-town in Steve's VW Golf, I peeked at the speedometer, and asked if he was afraid of getting a ticket. "Haven't gotten one yet," Steve said, then winked. Well, he might not have at that point, but it wasn't long after that that a police cruiser pulled us over. And it got worse. When the police car door opened, and I saw the big brown boots that rode up close to the knees, the dark pants and jacket, I almost gagged. A state trooper. Behind the state trooper's mirrored glasses was not a happy face. His mouth was in a scowl, and his stride was long and steady. He didn't even make an effort to lean down when he came to the open driver's side window.

"What's the hurry?" the officer asked in a deep, steady voice.

Steve leaned against the door and stuck his head out the window. "I'm real sorry, officer," he said. "We got to talking, and before I knew it we were going pretty fast. I didn't even realize it."

"We?" The officer squatted down and peered past Steve, who had moved his head to the side. "Where are you boys heading that you have to talk so much the driver can't concentrate on the road?"

"Home, sir," Steve said. "We're coming back from a weekend in P-town."

We were in for it now, or so I thought as I leaned forward to get a better look at the officer's face. But when I looked, it seemed as if the trooper had something bulging out between his legs that hadn't been there before.

"You and your friend?" the trooper asked.

"Yes, sir," Steve said. "It cost a lot of money, more than I had to spend, but it was worth it."

"I see," the officer said. "License and registration."

Steve pulled his wallet out of the back pocket of his shorts while I searched for the registration, pushing aside condoms, and small packets of lubricant. Finally I found the yellow registration card and handed it over. Steve held the documents close to the state trooper's meaty bulge. The trooper took them, then walked back to his patrol car.

"He'll probably have you stay here and wait," Steve said. "But if he happens to want to talk to the both of us, don't get in a panic."

I pulled down the visor and waited for the state trooper to get out of the car. When he did, his shaft was even more evident in his pants, the length running down his left thigh and shifting with each step. When he reached the car, he placed both hands on the roof, and looked inside once more. "Well, son, it seems you have a good driving record."

"I do, officer," Steve said. "It would suck if I got a ticket."

"I bet it would." The officer grinned, then looked past Steve. "Your friend must agree."

"I do, officer," I said nervously.

The state trooper shook his head. "If you boys want to talk about it, I just might be able to get rid of this for you. There's a rest area with a men's room just down the way. I can meet you guys there."

"Will do, sir," Steve said. Then, once the state trooper was out of the way, Steve turned to me and grinned. "We're golden."

I couldn't believe what was going on. Steve was going to get out of a speeding ticket, and I was helping. The officer followed us to the rest area, which wasn't even a mile down the highway. Once there, we both got out of the car and walked into the men's room, which to my amazement was vacant. None of the three stalls at the end had doors, and the floor near the row of three urinals was splotched with urine. I doubted any of the three sinks actually had running water. One of the sinks was tilted and the drain pipe was no longer connected.

The door opened and in stepped the state trooper, whose every footfall echoed through the tiled rest room. He stood in front of Steve, then unzipped his pants. "Okay, boy, let's talk about that ticket."

Steve dipped his hand inside the state trooper's fly, then pulled out his massive cock. The meaty tube of flesh rose up six inches, with a big purple knob. Turning, Steve motioned for me to join him.

"I don't have all day, there, boys," the trooper said.

Steve got to work, easing the statey's shaft into his mouth, then swallowing the entire length in one gulp. I was amazed that he didn't gag. That cock was real thick, but Steve had no problem stretching his lips around it, then easing it down his throat until his nose was buried in the trooper's wirey bush.

I couldn't just kneel there and do nothing, so I pulled out the trooper's balls, which were big and hairy. They hung low in their sack, and filled my mouth to capacity. I started by sucking one into my mouth, then taking in the other ball. With both nuggets in my mouth, I pulled down, and the trooper sighed and moaned.

"Suck that dick, boy," the trooper said.

My cock was swollen and eager for a little action, too. Pulling out my prick, I started stroking it. Steve was doing the same, using the spit that had collected around his mouth and dripped off as lube for his shaft.

"Oh, shit, man," the state trooper said. "I'm about to cum." Steve pulled his mouth off the guy's prick, then gripped his shaft. After a few strokes of his meat, the trooper shot his first load of spunk past Steve's face, and onto the wall. The second shot came just short of splattering on the wall, and the rest of his load shot onto the floor in front of us.

The state trooper held his prod when he was done creaming, then ran his index finger along the bottom of his shaft to squeeze out the final remains of spunk onto his fingers, which he then licked clean. "Don't let me catch you boys speeding again, you hear me?" he said.

"Yes, sir," Steve said.

After the state trooper left, Steve grabbed my shaft and I grabbed his. We pulled each others' puds until we shot our loads.

On the way back home, I asked Steve how he knew he could get out of that speeding ticket. Steve just shook his head, then said, "You call your own shots, and make your own luck. You have to believe in yourself, man. That's all it takes."

It was easy for Steve to think that way because he didn't know any other way. I mean, that statey probably took one look at Steve and couldn't help but see how nice his prick would look between those beautiful lips. Just walking around on campus during the school year, faculty and other students would always see Steve and wave hello. It seemed as if he knew everyone. He said it was only because he wasn't afraid to meet people head on and say hello. He said it isn't hard to be friendly.

And that was Steve's philosophy. He truly believed it had to do with his attitude. I thought he was naive.

Well, time moved on and Steve's roommate ended up moving in with his boyfriend. Steve asked if I wanted to share an off campus apartment with him, and I agreed. At first I wasn't sure how much work I would be able to get done living with Steve, but soon found out that he was a hard worker.

Once we were roommates, Steve really started to take me under his wing, reminding me to smile when we were on the street. Always look up, and don't watch your feet when you walk. Guys want to meet you, they just don't know it yet. I took everything he said with a grain of salt. After all, Steve didn't know what it was like to be average. Then something happened.

It happened while I was driving back from visiting my parents. I had left their house late, and wanted to make it to Providence before midnight. The highway was pretty empty, so I started doing seventy miles per hour, then found my speed increased to seventy-five. Not long after that I was pushing eighty. The highway stretched out, the headlights of my car illuminating the pavement. It was easy to speed. Eighty miles per hour didn't feel any different from fifty-five. I turned on the radio, relaxed, and drove.

Then I saw flashing lights behind me. With the volume on the radio turned down, the sound of the siren rung out in the night. I had been caught. Pulling over to the side of the road, I tried not to think about how much the speeding ticket would be. I didn't have more than enough for my share of next month's rent in the bank, I was not going to be able to pay a speeding ticket.

The cop's flashlight shone into the car, making it hard for me to see his face. "License and registration," the police officer said.

My license was easy, but when I went into the glove compartment to fish out the registration, a few condoms fell out.

"Everything okay in there?" the cop asked, the flashlight illuminating the interior of the car. That was when I saw the officer's face. His hair was cut military short, and his thin lips were almost in the shape of a grin, as if he was trying not to smile. He pulled his head away from the window as I sat back up, registration and license in hand.

Turning, I noticed the officer's cock was hard and outlined in his pants. I thought about Steve, and how he'd always told me to take risks, and to believe in myself. All I had to do was relax, and smile. I held the documents out to the officer, keeping them at crotch level.

"Do you know why I stopped you?" the officer asked.

"I was speeding, sir," I said. "It's not something I normally do. In fact, I've never had a speeding ticket before."

"Well, this could be your first," the policeman said. "They're not cheap, you know."

I met the officer's stare, then glanced down at his bulging crotch. "I really can't afford a ticket."

"Maybe you shouldn't have been speeding," he said, then scratched his bulging meat.

"I know, sir." I didn't know what to do next. He wasn't acting like the cop that had stopped me and Steve. I concentrated on breathing to stay calm. The officer did have a big hardon, that had to count for something.

The officer leaned in close to my ear. "You want to talk about this?"

My cock shot up good and stiff. "Can we?"

"Look, here's the deal," the policeman said. "You grab one of those condoms off the floor, and we'll walk to those bushes over there. What do you say?"

Like I was going to say no to that? I snagged the condom and a sample tube of lubricant, then met him behind the bushes. The cop pulled out his log, which had to be at least seven inches long. The shaft alone was so thick that the cop's fingers barely met when he wrapped them around it and waved it at me. I handed him the condom, then pulled down my pants. Let me tell you, my prick was damn hard just from the thought of having that cop fuck me up the ass.

"Bend over," the officer said. I did and he went down and spit on my fuck hole. Then I felt his tongue getting it all wet and ready for his massive prick. Reaching back, I spread my ass cheeks and let him go to town. He licked, then spat on my hole, pushing his fingers inside and spreading the hole open. He smeared more spit on my fuck hole, then finger fucked it a little more. Then he stopped, and I felt cold lubricant being smeared on my pucker. He pushed his thumbs inside. "You've got a fucking hot ass, boy."

The cop positioned the head of his cock against my hole, gently pressing until only the head was inside. He paused, then slowly eased his prick deep inside my bowels. My sphincter stretched wide to accommodate the girth of his massive rod. Never before had I had something so thick up my ass, and had to breathe deep and slow to keep my ass loose. Once inside, he grabbed my hips.

"You're so fucking tight," he said.

Looking down, I saw the cop's black boots between my parted legs. "Go slow," I said.

He pulled out until only the head of his cock was inside, then gradually slipped it back in. I spat in my hand, then grabbed my shaft. After only a few strokes, I felt enough jizm build up in the head that I knew it would shoot if I kept on it. And that cop was really giving me a nice slow fuck, easing his meat in and out of my fuck chute like he had all the time in the world.

"Go harder," I said.

The cop let out a grunt, then really started to give me his fuck stick good and hard. He pulled his shaft out of my ass, making my bowels feel empty, then slammed it inside in one fell swoop. I had to bite my lip to keep from crying out in pleasure. That cop knew how to fuck a guy, that was for sure.

It wasn't long before I felt the head of his prick swell up, getting ready to blow a hot load of spunk up my ass. "Oh yeah, man, you feel good," the cop said. That was when I put my hand back to my prick and started working it. After a few strokes, the cop slammed his shaft into my ass and his cock head started to pulse. He pulled half way out, then slammed in again. "Fuck," the cop whispered as his body shook. Once more he pulled out, then quickly shoved his meat back inside.

That was when I came. My ass clenched the cop's prick as the first and second shots exploded from my piss slit, landing on the ground. Gently, the cop pulled his prick out as I continued to empty my ball juice, trying to keep as quiet as possible, which was difficult.

Once finished, I stood on shaky legs and pulled up my pants. The cop tossed the condom, then grinned. "You've got one hot ass," he said.

I thanked him and we walked back to our cars. When I got back into the driver's seat, the interior was suddenly flooded with light, then went dark again. The cop had flashed his high beams at me. Peering into the rearview mirror, I saw that he had turned on his red and blue patrol car lights. Then the cop was getting out of the car, walking right to me. I couldn't believe that little fuck was going to give me a ticket after all! Nervously, I watched his approach from the driver's side mirror.

"Is something wrong, officer?" I said when he was in front of the door.

"Nothing at all," he said, handing me a piece of paper. "I just wanted to give you my phone number."

His phone number. I was floored.

After that I started acting different when on the street, or in a club. And I found that men started actually making time to talk to me, even if I wasn't with Steve. Steve even noticed the difference in me, and said he was happy to finally see me come out of my shell.

Steve wanted to know what had happened that had changed me so much, but for some reason I didn't want to share my cop story with him, so I just told him that he'd been right all along. A little self assurance can go a long way.

THE REAL THING

Drake Winslow woke up, grabbed his thick prick and gave it a jerk. His foreskin rose up over his cock head and hid the piss slit before he pulled his hand down and exposed the ripe knob with a drop of precum formed at the tip. He played peek a boo a few more times before grabbing his hairy balls and pulling down on them as he thought of Ian lying next to him, his hand resting against his chest as he leaned in close to kiss him. Man, he wanted something real, a big cock rubbing against his body. Drake felt his upper legs tighten as cum pressed against his cock head, getting ready to shoot. He gave his shaft another stroke and sprayed his funk over his stomach.

Drake grabbed the towel he kept on the bed and wiped the jizm off his stomach, sat up and slid his ass to the side of the bed and into the wheelchair at the bedside. He used the keypad set into the right armrest to wheel himself out of the bedroom and down the hall to the bathroom. "Max, get the shower ready," Drake said.

"Confirmed." Max's deep, male voice came through the speakers set into the ceiling. "Plans for the new Osaka Mall are due tomorrow."

Drake wheeled into the white tiled bathroom and closed the sliding door. Once the armrest of the wheel chair was lowered he was able to move from the wheelchair to the plastic shower chair with a simple slide to the left. The shower chair was low enough for him to roll to the steady spray of water across the room.

It had been just over a year since he'd lost the movement of his legs to the Osaka earthquake. He'd been visiting the site for the mall not far from the Sumiyushi Grand Shrine, its ancient red and black buildings being dwarfed by the monolithic black pillars rising into the air around it. The Sumiyushi Grand Shrine had been placed under a clear dome to keep it free from the pollutants that plagued the city. When the earthquake had hit, everyone who had been standing on the mall site had stood still and looked quizzically at one another as if they had been cartoon characters. Then buildings had begun to collapse and screams rose out amongst the sound of the trembling earth. Rubble from a toppling building had fallen onto the mall site, sending Drake, his co-workers and the mall investors fleeing from flying debris. The siding of a building had hit Drake's legs, toppling him down to the ground and causing him to lose feeling in his lower body. When the quake had ended, all that could be heard were car alarms and sirens ringing out through clouds of billowing smoke. In the smog, there had been the shimmer of the clear dome that covered the Sumiyushi Grand Shrine. It had been saved.

The Osaka earthquake had killed over four thousand people, leaving hundreds injured.

Drake hadn't looked into getting cybergenic implants for his legs until he'd arrived back in L.A. DataCross Insurance had sent him a reply saying that such a procedure is considered a vanity operation and is not covered under his insurance policy. It hadn't been until then that Drake had understood the rash of insurance company bombings that had taken place back in the spring of 2015.

Drake's office was down the hall from the bathroom with windows that caught the rising sun between two neighboring buildings looming a good twenty stories above his thirty-second story apartment. Sitting in front of his desk, the light from the desk size touch pad illuminated Drake's face. He looked down at the blueprint of the Osaka Mall that he'd been working on all week. Using the track ball set on the side of the touch pad, he manipulated the plan, making the diagrammed outline of the mall turn so he could view it from every angle. He'd drawn special absorption pads along the outer edge of each floor, and spring joints that could be set into motion by the building's main computer in case of another earthquake. His only problem now was finding the best area to store the main frame and figure out how low he would have to sink the tremor bar into the ground.

Drake looked up at the picture he'd had Max print out from a skin mag. "You are allowed this function only once, are you sure you want to print this out?" Max had said. Drake had rolled his eyes, wishing he could take the legality feature out of the MagView program. The picture was of two muscular men, one on his knees with the other man's massive cock plunged halfway down his throat. He liked the picture because it reminded him of the life he'd had before the quake in Osaka. Back when he used to cruise the dark alleys on ground level, moving between buildings where men and boys stood around waiting for someone to take them into a side door or one of the many indentations set into the sides of the buildings. He still remembered the boy with the holographic tattoo of Poseidon rising up from the sea with a big, thick piece of meat between his legs and low hanging balls. The guy had been kissing Drake's mouth once he'd shoved him against the side of the building. Drake had felt his hands unbutton his jeans and lug out his meat. The guy had gone down on his knees and had started sucking Drake's fuck stick, sliding the flat of his tongue against the under side of his shaft as he swallowed his prick. Drake had placed his hands on either side of his head and started ramming his prick in and out of his mouth, getting himself all excited and wanting to fuck his ass real good.

Drake had felt cum rising in his shaft, but had not wanted to blow his load yet. He'd pulled his cock out of his mouth and rubbed the slab of stiff meat against his face. "No, I don't want to cum yet," Drake had said.

"Yeah, what you want then?" the guy had said, giving Drake a cocky grin.

"Pull down your pants and let me take a look at your ass," Drake had said.

"You got a glove?" The guy had pulled his pants down and had placed his hands on the wall, exposing his firm ass cheeks.

"You bet." He'd unrolled a condom onto his prick and gave it a few strokes, feeling the cum rising up his shaft once more. Drake had reached around the guy's waist and grabbed hold of his thick cock. He'd run his hand over the shaft, feeling the ripe cock head before starting to give the shaft a few smooth strokes. Precum had drooled out of the guy's piss slit and onto the ground. Drake had moved his hand away from the cock. "Stroke it while I fuck you," he'd said.

"Sure man."

Drake had pressed his cock head against the guy's pucker, feeling the tight hole open to greet his shaft. The guy's bowels had been tight and warm as Drake smoothed his shaft in and out of his fuck hole. The guy had sighed and groaned. "Oh man," the guy had said, "your cock feels so good. Fuck me, man. Give it to me." Drake had let himself blow his load right there, with his pole buried deep in the man's bowels.

Drake wished he could be there again, standing on two legs and fucking some punk against the side of a building. He looked down at the mall plans, closed the file and logged onto the InfoNet Research Center to find out how far he needed to sink the tremor bar into the ground.

The phone outlet in the bedroom was a safe place for Drake to jack into. Drake took off his shirt, then moved from the wheel chair to the bed. Once on the bed he was able to pull off his pants and socks. He grabbed the Virtual Reality glasses and assorted Velcro cuffs and placed them on the bed with their wires untangled. His cock was already hard as he pulled off his pants, rising up and bouncing in the air like an excited friend. Drake wrapped the metallic Velcro cloth around his shaft, then plugged it into the black box that housed the hard drive, CD drive and software, known as the CPU. He set the clear jizm flask over his cock head, then slid the finger cups onto each finger tip and connected the thin wires that trailed off the small finger cups into the CPU. He taped the bands that go around his legs to his waist. If he wanted his legs to move in Virtual Reality all he would have to do was move his upper torso. The VR glasses gave a crisp, clear image and had a set of headphones set into the sides of the glasses. Drake put on the glasses and pressed the red button on the CPU.

A blue screen with the Comdon logo rose up in thick, gold letters, shimmered, then faded out to blue as the CPU booted up. The screen turned black, then lit up to show the monitor. Computer program icons were to his left, a trash can to his right. He reached out and tapped the icon to dial up the remote host to get onto the net, then waited. He'd already set the coordinates to access Ian's site on connect. There was a ring, letting Ian know that he had connected to the host computer.

A window appeared that said, Choose your avatar. Drake had a choice of three avatars that he'd made. Two of the avatars had buff bodies and hairless chests. The only difference between the two of them was that one was more tan than the other. The third avatar was a duplicate of himself, without the wheel chair, wearing a pair of blue boxer shorts. He'd made the avatar from a photograph of himself. Whenever he was with Ian he used his real image avatar, as did Ian.

The monitor went white, then the walls faded in. A king sized bed came into view. "Welcome to Ian's site, how can I help you?" a deep, male voice said.

Drake was silent. A dark, muscular man appeared to his left, wearing tight jeans that accented his massive crotch. Drake had never seen the man before, and assumed he was a specially designed robot program, or bot as most people call them. "Who are you?" Drake asked.

"The keeper," the same male voice said. The image file was out of sync with the sound file, an easy enough problem to fix. "Do you have an appointment?"

"Yes."

"Your name please."

"Drake."

"I will now scan your coordinates for your IP address and server."

Drake waited.

"Your server is secured," the keeper said. "One moment please."

The keeper stepped back against the wall as Ian appeared, dressed in a silk robe that covered his body. Drake knew that under the robe was a small belly and a chest that was firming down and could use some daily exercise. Drake didn't mind, since it was an honest body, something real. He found it a pleasant change from the perfect bodies of the avatars, with their rippling muscles and perfect skin. Drake's body was honest too, to a degree. He'd made it so his avatar's legs worked, which made him feel dishonest if he thought about it, which he didn't do that often.

"How have you been?" Ian asked, his English accent thick.

"Good, but I have to leave Friday for Tokyo. Don't know if I can find a secure place to jack in, or if I'll ever have time."

"They don't sleep in Tokyo," Ian said.

"They can't afford to sleep, especially with the market still hurting."

Silence.

"Nice bot, by the way," Drake said.

"Still have to get the voice to match up with the lips. Picked him up a few days ago. Figure it should take an hour or so to get that lined up."

Ian walked up to Drake, slipped his hand around his waist.

Their lips met briefly. "How long will you be gone?" Ian asked.
"Five days, if all goes well. I'll keep in contact with you. I don't
need a secure jack to send mail. We just can't do this." Drake
slipped his hand between the opening of the robe. All manner of
touch had been programmed into the avatar, giving Drake the sensation of touching skin.

Ian slipped his hands into Drake's briefs and pulled them down.
"Maybe we could meet," Ian said. "We've known each other for
over a year now."

Drake thought about meeting Ian. He'd wanted to before, had
even had jerk off sessions thinking of him, but didn't want to risk
being rejected because of his legs. "It wouldn't be the same," Drake
said. "We would have to use condoms. This way is safer, nothing to remember."

"It isn't real," Ian said.

"But it feels real," Drake said as he reached down and grabbed
hold of Ian's shaft, feeling electrical impulses move through his
body, duplicating touch and weight. "You're here in front of me.
I can see you. Everything." He slid his hand down the hard shaft
and cupped his fingers around his ball sack. "And it feels so damn
good." He pushed his middle finger under his nuts, following the
thin strand of flesh leading to his tight fuck hole. "I can do things
this way." He felt the puckered opening with the tip of his finger
and pressed.

Ian's robe fell off his shoulders and landed on the floor. "It's
true," Ian said as the two men lowered themselves onto the bed.
They kissed deeply, their tongues pushing into each others' mouths
as their hands moved over their simulated bodies. Yes, it was close
to real, but not real enough.

He couldn't help but wonder how much better Ian would feel
in person, naked before him. Ian's body moved down Drake's
body. There was warmth on his cock head and he looked down.
Ian's head was there, moving up and down on his shaft. Yes, it
felt good, but how much better would it feel to have the real thing?
Drake put his hands behind his back, feeling the simulated suck
on his prick. He knew he was about to blow his load, he could
feel the surging cum rising up his shaft, filling his cock head and
getting ready to burst.

Ian stopped sucking Drake's cock and looked up at him. He

moved up Drake's torso and kissed him on the lips. "I want to feel you for real. Have you fuck me for real."

Drake was silent.

"Is it because of the earthquake in Osaka? I know you were there at the time. You said you were working on the new mall."

Drake reached out and touched Ian's arm. The electrical impulses moving through his fingers were close to warmth, something almost like flesh. For a moment Drake wished that Ian was with him, in the flesh. "Can we talk about this later?" Drake said. "I want to see you sit on my prick."

"Sure," Ian said, positioning himself on Drake's cock. Drake watched as Ian reached behind himself, probably getting a dildo ready to push into his ass as he moved up and down on the image of Drake's stiff prick. Drake felt warmth engulfing his cock as he watched Ian sit on his avatar's shaft and begin to move up and down. Ian was jerking his prick as he rode Drake's meat. This is so close to the real thing, Drake thought as he leaned back, feeling cum rising in his shaft, collecting at the swollen knob. Ian's head fell back as his hips lurched forward. A jet stream of hot cum pulsed out of Ian's ripe knob and arched over Drake's head, hitting the wall in splattering globs. Drake closed his eyes as he felt his body contract. He let out a groan and shot his load into the clear latex bulb that engulfed his cock head.

When Drake opened his eyes, the room was filled with thin strands of swirling colors. "Pretty cool, huh?" Ian said.

Drake smiled. "Sure is."

"So, what do you say? Why don't we meet when you get back from Osaka?"

"Let me think about it," Drake said.

"Sure."

"I have to go." Drake stood up and walked across the room, towards the exit sign. The screen faded to white.

From: Drake458@bts.net
To: IanG@idnet.net
Subject: meeting
Date sent: Thu, 15 Jan 2245 19:06:24

Ian,

I've decided to tell you the truth. As you have
suspected, I have lost the use of my legs during
the Osaka quake. If you still would like to meet,
let me know. I will be back home next Thursday.

Drake

Drake was sitting at his desk. The Osaka Mall construction was
due to begin the following month. "A man named Ian is at the
door. Would you like visual confirmation?" Max said.

"Yes."

The desk screen flickered onto a picture of Ian in a dark jacket
standing in front of the door. "Open the door for him, Max."

Drake wheeled out of the office and into the hall, heading
towards the entryway where Ian was waiting for him. "Here I am,"
Drake said.

"Yes, here you are," Ian said, then gave Drake a kiss on the lips.
"Nice place." Ian's shaft was pressing out against the inside of his
pants.

"Should I show you the place now or later?"

"Later," Ian said, placing his hand between Drake's legs and feeling his stiffening cock. "How about we get down to business?"

"Follow me."

It wasn't long before Ian and Drake were undressed and on the
bed. Ian's cock was long and stiff, exactly as it looked in Virtual
Reality. Drake held it in his grip, feeling the warmth and stiffness.
Ian leaned over and kissed Drake full on the lips. Their mouths
opened to greet each others' tongues, suck on them and taste each
others' mouths. Ian rolled on top of Drake and rubbed his hard
cock against his flesh. Ian felt warm and comforting. Drake felt
his shaft pressed against Ian's body. This is it, he thought. Ian
started licking his nipple, gently biting on the tip before sliding his
lips down his chest and wrapping his lips around his bulbous
knob. Ian's mouth was warm and moist as he swallowed every
inch of his shaft.

Drake closed his eyes as Ian pulled on his big, hairy nuts as his
head bobbed up and down on his rod. He reached down and

pulled his cock out of Ian's mouth. "I don't want to cum yet," he said.

"Sure," Ian said as he crawled up to Drake and sat with his balls hanging in his face. Drake opened his mouth and sucked them into his mouth, rolling them over his tongue before popping them out and licking beneath them. He reached around Ian's legs and held onto his firm ass cheeks, spreading them apart and feeling the crack of his ass with the tips of his fingers. Ian moved his ass forward and Drake inhaled the musty scent of his ass before sticking out his tongue and giving the tight pucker a lick. He put the tip of his finger against his fuck hole and pressed, feeling his ass ring open.

My shaft would feel good up his ass, he thought as he pushed another finger into the tight hole and spread it open before him. "I want to fuck you," Drake said.

"I would love that," Ian said. "You have a condom?"

Drake reached over to the night stand and grabbed a condom from the top drawer, along with a tube of lubricant. Ian watched as Drake unrolled the latex glove onto his shaft and lubed it up.

"I've been wanting to feel you up my ass for so long," Ian said as he positioned himself over Drake's ripe knob and slowly sat down on it.

Ian's ass ring gripped Drake's shaft, holding it in a tight caress as he lowered himself onto his prick. It felt better than VR, Drake thought as he watched Ian slide up and down his stiff pole as he stroked his prick.

Once more Drake knew that he was about to cum. He felt the thick fuck fluids building up at the head of his prick, begging for release. He wanted this fuck to last, to keep his cock buried deep inside Ian's fuck chute for as long as possible.

"Oh shit," Ian hissed as a thick wave of hot jizm spewed from his piss slit and splattered over Drake's neck, then another hit his collar bone and more sprayed onto his chest. Ian sprayed his funk on Drake's chest as he continued to ride his pole. It wasn't long before Drake felt his legs tighten and his shaft shoot its creamy load up Ian's ass.

When Drake had finished coming, Ian rose and spread out on the bed next to him. Drake pulled off the condom and threw it in the basket across the room. "It has been so long since I've done anything like that," he said.

"We can do this again."

Drake sat up. "You don't have to say that."

"No shit," Ian said as he reached out and pulled Drake on top of him. He gave him a kiss. "I don't have to say or do anything."

Drake was silent. He felt Ian's cock stiffening against his stomach. "Well, it is better than VR sex," he said.

THE MEN OF THE HOUSE

It was late in the autumn of 1835 that found me traveling in the wake of a tumultuous storm. I was on my way to Providence to visit an old friend. It was mid day, and already the sky had become filled with dark clouds. Strong winds had begun to form, forcing me to search for shelter in a still unsettled portion of land miles from my destination. That was when I found the elaborate wrought iron gates with the family name Usher set into the top of the arched opening.

I guided my trusted steed through the gate, and up the path leading to the mansion ahead. The mansion was enormous, with three gables and a set of double doors. Due to the peeling paint and rotted clapboard on the exterior of the house, I assumed that it might not be inhabited. Above the gables of the three-story mansion, clouds began to swirl, and a bolt of lightning lit the sky.

Dismounting my steed, I kept hold of the reins and walked him up the cobblestone path leading to the double doors at the entrance to the house. If there were any occupants, I hoped they would be kind to a weary traveler. After a single rap upon the door, it was opened by a young man in a white starched shirt and black knickers. His eyes were as dark as his black hair, and his full lips curved into a grin. The boy looked to be just an inch or so shy of my height, and his frame was slender. And, dare I say so early in this tale, between his legs displayed a hint of arousal which he did not attempt to hide from my view.

"I am traveling to Providence, and am seeking shelter from the storm that is brewing," I said.

The young man glanced past my form. "Come inside, please," he said.

"If it would be no trouble to the master of the house," I said.

The boy's dark eyes met my gaze as he wetted his lips. "Then I shall take your steed to the stables." He stepped aside and motioned for me to enter. "Wait here."

The heels of my shoes clicked against the white marbled floor. In front of me wound a staircase that curved along the edge of the wall, the railings made from thick wood. At the far end of the room stood an urn of five feet that appeared to be from the Orient.

A crystal chandelier hung from the arched ceiling, and emitted a dull glow, for not all the candles sitting in its holders had been lit. I thought the low lighting might be an attempt to hide the age of the floral wallpaper, which, on close inspection appeared slightly yellowed. Or to hide the slight wear evident by the dull shine of the railing.

Then, from the entrance to my left there appeared a tall gentleman with dark hair, and a mustache. Dressed in a dark suit, he appeared the perfect gentleman standing with his hands behind himself. His eyes were a haunting emerald green, and seemed inviting and warm. Slowly, he extended his right hand towards me, then bowed. "I am Roderick Usher, master of the house," he said.

I told him of my journey, the approaching storm and my need for shelter. "If it is any trouble for me to stay here, sir, I will kindly make my way and find other means of warmth and shelter."

Roderick tilted back his head and let out a hearty laugh. "Do you take me for a bastard, my good man? Please, stay the night, or until the storm passes. I can show you to our guest rooms, where you may freshen up and rest."

I followed Roderick up the staircase, and into a long hall with hardwood floors. Paintings of men, all of whom had the same chiseled facial features and haunting eyes as Roderick Usher, hung upon the walls and watched our movements. Finally Roderick stopped at the last door on the left, then turned to me and gripped the handle. "I do hope you find this room appealing." And with that said, Roderick opened the door and followed me inside.

The room was more splendid than any in which I had ever stayed. The mahogany four-post bed had a canopy of royal blue that matched the silk sheets, and in the hearth there roared a fire that warmed the interior. To the right of where I stood was a closet standing on four claw-like legs. I stood in front of the closet and ran my hand along the fine woodwork.

"You find this room desirable?" Roderick said, his dark eyebrows raised.

"Very much so," I said, then noticed the painting to the left of the closet, which was of a naked young man whose pale body was thin and hairless, save the dark bush of pubic hair above his well endowed member, which hung limp between his legs. The hood of the boy's shaft covered the bulbous head and tapered to a small enclosure. The boy in the painting looked very much like Roderick, and at first I wondered if perhaps it was. Between my legs I felt my own member begin to stir, and hoped it would not be noticed.

"That is Matthew," Roderick said as he gently placed his hand upon my shoulder. "His chamber is down the hall, to the right, just opposite my own."

"Are there any others in the house?" I asked.

Roderick stepped away from me, then lowered his gaze as he gently ran the tips of his fingers over the smooth dark doors of the closet. "There are no others," he said, then stopped his motions and turned towards me. A long tubular bulge ran down Roderick's left thigh, and, despite my attempt to meet his gaze, I could not help but make furtive glances down at it.

"I am sorry," I said.

"Such things," Roderick said, dusting the air with his fingers. "My family lives to entertain. But there have been no parties for five years." Roderick looked up at Matthew's image in the frame and a playful grin spread over his face. "I remember the times of parties, when men visited and music filled the halls. How bold the Usher men were, they all said. But they were all so frightened of discovery. Nobody knew they visited our mirthful house." The tubular protrusion that ran down Roderick's left thigh became more evident. Roderick shifted his stance, and the bulge shifted and swayed with him.

"It all ended?" I said.

"Yes, it did." Roderick stepped up to the window and looked out. "This was once such a magical and beautiful place."

I stood next to Roderick and looked out at the back lawn, with its overgrown, misshapen bushes. Roderick placed his hand on the small of my back, and it felt as if there was a sadness emanating from his person. "Why did it end?" I asked.

"Silliness," Roderick said in a whisper. "Paranoia and fear of discovery. Such nonsense." Roderick patted my buttocks, then turned towards the room and let out a sigh. "But I am becoming morbid for no reason. Matthew and I would like it if you would join us for drinks in the drawing room."

"I would like that," I said.

Roderick grinned. "Very good. In the closet you will find some

clothes in your size. I will send my boy Stephen up to get you."
And with that, Roderick Usher left.

I thought about Roderick's words, and the painting hanging in
the room as I undressed. The house had been left to ruin because
Roderick no longer entertained. It seemed like such a waste, and
a shame. Sitting on the bed, feeling the fresh sheets beneath my
skin, and glancing at the painting on the wall, made my penis
stiffen once more.

There was a rap upon the door, then I heard a voice call out to
me, asking if I needed assistance. Quickly, I grabbed a pillow from
the head of the bed and used it to cover my nakedness. "Come in,"
I said.

The door opened, and in walked the boy who had taken my
horse to the stables. The boy's shaft was clearly evident in his
knickers, as were his testicles. "Master Roderick sent me up to
you," the boy said.

"You must be Stephen," I said, feeling a blush rise to my cheeks.

"You will need a change of clothes for tonight," Stephen said.
"Please, stand."

I stood, keeping the pillow in front of my lower half to hide my
excitement.

Stephen reached for the pillow. "Please, if you don't mind. I've
seen naked men before." He grinned and met my gaze. "Many
times before."

I allowed this young man to take the pillow away, and saw his
eyes widen when they fell upon my erection. "You have nothing
to be ashamed of," Stephen said, reaching out and wrapping his
warm fingers around my shaft. He moved in closer. "It is quite
lovely." And with that, Stephen went down on his knees and
slipped his tongue inside my foreskin and around my swollen
knob. I closed my eyes and enjoyed the intoxicating pleasure of
the boy's warm, moist mouth and the pull of his lips. I placed my
hands on his head, pushing my fingers through his silky hair.
Stephen grabbed hold of my balls and gently pulled down on them.

It wasn't long before my legs began to give way, and I knew that
soon my frothy countenance would fill the boy's mouth. I let out
a grunt, then felt the first blast shoot from my rod. Stephen swallowed. The second and third shots rang out, and the boy hungrily
gulped down every last drop of my load.

Stephen extracted my member from his mouth and wiped his lips with his palm. "We must get you dressed," he said, then walked to the closet.

"Stephen," I asked, "how long have you been employed by the Ushers?"

Stephen pulled a white shirt from out of the closet and held it up as if sizing it to my torso. "I have been with the Ushers since birth. My mother was the cook, and my father drove their carriages. Why do you ask?"

"You remember the parties, then," I said.

"Yes, they were splendid, indeed," Stephen said. He handed me the shirt, and I slipped it on. "The men were so handsome, and virile. And the grounds, how spectacular they were then. Everything was as it should be." He turned back and sorted through the clothes hanging inside the closet.

"And how long has it been since the grounds keepers were let go?" I asked.

"The masters of the house do not like such talk," Stephen said. "Rumors and scandal had once fallen upon the house, and never will again." Stephen studied a pair of black slacks. He brushed off some lint from the leg, then held them out for me to take. "But it would be nice to see things back to how their great grandfather had set them. 'A party enchants a home with life,' he once said."

I stepped into the slacks, then buttoned up the front flap.

"Sebastian Usher," Stephen said. "His portrait hangs in the hall with the other Usher men. I am only thankful they are not alive to see what has befallen their dream."

When I reached the drawing room, I heard the soft melody being played on the dark wood pianoforte. At first glance I thought it was Roderick sitting behind the pianoforte, but found that Roderick was lounging on the chaise in front of the hearth. Both men wore matching gray suits, with white shirts. "You have not yet met Matthew," Roderick said, taking the snifter of amber liquid out from under his nose and holding it in front of himself.

"It's a pleasure to meet you," Matthew said without stopping his playing. "I hope you enjoy your stay with us."

I looked around the room, which was spacious, with dark green walls and a black and white marble floor that helped the music fill the space. Behind the pianoforte were three windows that ran from floor to ceiling and looked out over the overgrown hedges in the back yard. Thin white cloth was draped over a rod at the top of each window and hung to the floor on either side. A sofa faced the chaise lounge, and a matching chair. In front of the sofa was a table which held crystal containers filled with assorted liqueurs and brandies. A snifter of an amber liquid sat on the pianoforte, and there was an empty snifter and a pony on the table amongst the containers. At the far left of the room, against a set of double doors that led to the back of the house, was a statue of a man in a classical pose. The figure's penis was rather large, and the foreskin covered only half the head.

"Please, join us in a drink," Roderick said. "Something to take away the chill of this horribly damp evening." Roderick stood and picked up a container. "Perhaps some brandy will help?"

I nodded approval, and Roderick poured some brandy into the snifter and held it out to me. I swirled the liquid, then lifted the snifter to my nose and inhaled the subtle essence of the brandy.

"We do enjoy having company," Matthew said as he stepped away from the pianoforte, placing his bulging endowment in perfect view. He studied my form, then walked directly up to me and brushed some lint off my shoulder.

"Those clothes compliment your form," Roderick said. "You should take them with you."

Matthew moved towards the windows near the pianoforte and looked out at the dark sky. He took a sip from his snifter, then let out a sigh. "It's going to rain soon, or so it appears."

"Come away from the window," Roderick said. "Let's not be sorrowful, especially in the midst of such dashing company."

A burst of lightning quickly lit the room, followed by a clap of thunder. Then heavy rain fell and beat upon the ground, slapping the windows on the eastern side of the house. Roderick expelled air from between his full lips, then slowly shook his head. His hands smoothed my back, stopped at the outward curve of my buttocks.

"Alas, if things were different we would not have the pleasure of your company," Roderick said. "Perhaps tomorrow the clouds will lift and you can find it in your heart to stay longer."

I placed my hand on the small of Matthew's back. Matthew's

warm breath brushed against my neck as he moved back, then pressed his lips against mine. My cock stiffened as our mouths opened, and he gently sucked my tongue.

Then Roderick was behind me, his hands slipping around my waist, unfastening the buttons on my shirt, then sliding up and undoing the knot of my tie. My lips parted from Matthew's, then he stepped back and unfastened my pants. Roderick slipped my shirt off as I kicked off my shoes, and allowed my slacks to fall. My stiff dick was in front of Matthew's face, and he grabbed onto my balls and sucked them into his mouth.

The fire in the hearth sent a warm, flickering glow throughout the room as the storm outside heightened its fury. Roderick undressed as Matthew grabbed my shaft and slowly stroked its length. I watched as Roderick let his white shirt and black tie fall to the floor. Roderick's chest was smooth, his pectorals beautifully defined with dark nipples accenting the outer corners. His lower torso tapered down to his waist, where his slacks began. The firm tube of flesh that was evident between Roderick's legs was soon to be exposed as he unbuttoned them and let them fall to his feet. His shaft was thicker than any I had ever seen, and seemed to be at least nine inches in length, with foreskin that covered the head and tapered at the tip.

Roderick regained his position behind me, bringing his hands around my torso once more and rubbing my hard nipples with his thumbs. I felt Roderick's stiffening shaft against my ass, slipping into the crack as his hands smoothed my torso. As Roderick's fingers pushed through my wiry bush of pubic hair, Matthew stood and began to undress.

Roderick's thick fingers gripped my shaft, and the tip of his tongue moved up my neck, towards my ear. I closed my eyes and felt Roderick nibble upon the edge of my right earlobe as he pulled down on my prick, bringing my foreskin back and exposing the ripe head of my cock. Then my knob was engulfed in warmth, and moisture. I looked down to find Matthew, naked and on his knees, slipping my entire rod down his throat. It was such a pleasure to have these two handsome men touching and kissing my flesh.

Roderick stopped kissing my neck and went down on his knees. He parted my ass cheeks, then began to lick the hole. His moist tongue poked at the tight opening, then pushed inside as Matthew continued his ministrations on my fleshy pole.

I heard the door open, then Stephen stepped inside. He, too, was unclothed. In Stephen's upturned left hand was an oval silver tray, upon which sat a small glass jar of ointment. Stephen held the tray out to Roderick, who took the jar and placed it on the floor by his side. Stephen then went and took a seat upon the chair on which Roderick had been sitting when I first entered the chamber.

A burst of lightning lit the room, followed by a clap of thunder. A soft, low moan spread through the house as I felt Roderick slather the ointment on my asshole. Then the knobby head of Roderick's prick pressed against the tight hole and he slowly pushed until my ass ring widened to accommodate the girth of his fuck stick. Matthew stood, and Roderick's shaft slowly slid back and forth inside my bowels.

Matthew's lips gently brushed past mine. "Help us bring life back into this old house," he said, then reached behind me to touch Roderick.

I smoothed my palms over Matthew's form, feeling the curve of his ass. Roderick's meat slipped out of my hole until it felt as if only the head was encased by my flesh, then he pushed it back inside, inch by inch. I had to breathe slow and steady to keep from clenching my hole. Matthew reached between my legs and slipped one finger along either side of Roderick's pistoning rod.

"He's fucking you," Matthew whispered.

Roderick was fucking my ass, and it felt good. Sperm began to build up in the head of my shaft, driving me wild with lust. I tried to touch myself, but Matthew batted my hand away.

"Not yet," Matthew said. "We want to fill you with our cream." Then Matthew moved to the side, and kissed Roderick.

Roderick's breath became heavy, and I felt the head of his fleshy tube swell and scrape against my bowels. Then he let out a grunt. He gripped my hips, and thrust his meat deep inside with one quick plunge. And that was when I felt the head of Roderick's prick swell, then pulse. Hot spunk shot into my hole, filling me with his seed.

Stephen sat in the chair, his legs extended as he casually ran the tips of his fingers along the length of his stiff dick. A grin spread over his handsome face as Roderick slipped his column out of my hole, and Matthew stepped behind me. It was with little effort on my part that Matthew was able to slip his thick cock inside my freshly used hole.

Roderick's pole was semi-hard as he stepped in front of me. He slipped his hand around the back of my neck, guiding me to bend and take his flesh between my lips to suckle the last of his sweet nectar. Then Roderick slipped his tube out from between my lips and allowed me to stand as Matthew fucked my ass.

I cannot tell you how eager I was to shoot my load. First Roderick had used my ass, then Matthew. The feeling of both these men slipping their poles in and out of my tight hole, massaging my insides like no man had ever done, caused me to be in such a state that thick preseminal fluids spilled from the tip of my dick and collected on the floor in a small puddle. Once more I made an attempt to take hold of my member, but Roderick would not allow it.

"Then take it in your mouth," I said to Roderick. Matthew's flesh was already swelling deep inside my body, and I knew it would not be long before it began to spew its froth.

Stephen stood, then padded across the floor to where we stood. The boy placed his hand upon my hip, then leaned forward and kissed Matthew. Matthew let out a grunt, then pulled back, only to push forward and bury his cock inside my ass once more. I felt the first wave of Matthew's sperm shoot inside my bowels, then the second. Then Matthew stopped his movements and let loose with the remainder of his juice until he was spent.

Stephen slipped down between my legs and began to lick the outer rim of my asshole as Matthew slipped his pole out of my bowels. Once Matthew's rod was extracted, Stephen knelt down where the man had stood to fuck me, and pressed his palms against my ass cheeks. Stephen's tongue slid in and out of my hole as it shrunk back to its original size. The mixture of the two men's spunk dribbled down my fuck chute and onto Stephen's tongue as he greedily lapped up their creamy seed.

Both Roderick and Matthew went down on their knees in front of me. I felt their tongues running along the sides of my shaft, then their lips kissing the very top of my swollen knob. A hand pulled back my skin, then the tip of a tongue tickled the underside of my stiff flesh. Looking down, I saw the two men kissing, the head of my member pressed between their lips. Behind me, Stephen pressed his lips against my hole and greedily pushed his tongue inside. I could hold back no longer. I shot my seed into both men's mouths, watching as each attempted to swallow the frothy blasts. The two men were not always successful in their attempts, and thick globs of white spunk fell onto their chins and cheeks.

When I had finished spewing my load, I stepped back. Stephen made haste to lick the excess spunk from his masters' faces before each of the three men stood before me. A collective sigh seemed to emanate from the very walls of the house, but I seemed to be the only person to notice. Outside, the storm began to fade. I took a seat upon the sofa, then fell into a blissful sleep.

The next morning I awoke in the guest room, naked and warm, tucked in between the soft cotton sheets of the guest room bed. Light streamed inside from the windows, and lit the room in a cheerful glow. Looking at the walls, I noticed the once yellow wallpaper appeared fresh and clear in the morning light.

Stephen knocked upon my door, then asked to enter.

"Please do," I said.

"A bath will be drawn if you would like," Stephen said.

"Yes, I would like that very much," I said.

"Also, both Sir Roderick and Sir Matthew have extended an open invitation for you to come and visit any time you feel fit," Stephen said, then walked to the closet and took out a purple silk robe for me to slip into. He placed the robe on the bed. "And now I will draw you a bath."

Getting up from bed, I walked to the window and looked out. The lawn that had been burnt the day prior was now lush and green. In the distance were well trimmed bushes in the shapes of a giraffe, an elephant, and a tiger.

A few feet in front of these bushes Roderick stood talking to Matthew, each man dressed fitting to his position in life. Roderick looked up and saw me standing naked in the window. He smiled and greeted me with a wave.

Stepping back to the bed, I slipped on the robe, feeling the cool material drift over my arms and buttocks. I stepped out of my room and into the hall, which smelled of fresh flowers. I padded past the paintings of the Usher men, and to the stairwell, which appeared freshly polished. I heard the clicking of heels against the marble floor down below, then saw Roderick's enchanting emerald eyes looking up at me.

"I do hope you take us up on our offer to visit," Roderick said. "It would be so nice to see the house alive again."

It was then that I knew I would come back to visit, and perhaps even bring a friend.

CONSTRUCTION MEN IN HEAT

Tony threw his yellow hard hat onto the passenger seat of his navy blue Ford Truck, climbed into the driver's seat, then slammed the door closed. Leaning back, he tried to think of something that would make his hardon go down. The fucker had been rubbing against the inside of his faded jeans all day, and he'd seen a few of the guys on the construction site try not to look at it. It was all that new guy's fault, Vince. Vince was so fucking gorgeous, with deep brown eyes and a firm ass. His hair was a soft brown, and his lower jaw had the rough stubble of a day's growth. And by the end of the day, Vince's thread-bare t-shirt had clung to him from the sweat of hard work, making his well defined pecs and firm stomach even more evident than when he'd walked on the site first thing in the morning. And Vince had been packing a pretty hefty bulge between his legs, too. He probably wore underwear, though. His meat didn't seem to wander down his leg or anything, unlike Tony's.

All day Tony had found it hard not to sneak a few looks at Vince. Four stories up, the two of them secured beams together until the support structure for the new building had been completed. It had been hard for Tony to keep his mind on his work. Thoughts of stuffing Vince's ass full of his dick kept finding their way into his head, and once inside he hadn't had a chance in the world of getting them out. And his prick just kept rubbing against the inside of his jeans, getting more and more stiff as time went on. He was thankful his dick didn't drool much precum like some guys' did. But still, he'd been afraid of getting so excited that he'd blow his load right in his jeans. What would he have done then? How would he have explained it? Nobody at the construction company knew he was gay. And as much as he could tell, he was the only gay guy on the entire site. Tony fought the urge to rub his shaft, despite the ache in his balls.

There was a pounding on his door that made Tony jump. Lenny stood outside the driver's side door grinning, which caused his bushy blond mustache to look longer than it was. He used his left hand to shade his blue eyes from the sun.

"Been a hard day?" Lenny said.

"Tired," Tony said, rubbing his left pectoral, although it wasn't sore. At least not yet. "Couldn't sleep last night."

"You got someone keeping you up?"

"Not that I know of," Tony said, pressing his foot down on the clutch and getting the truck in gear. "Now if you don't mind, I need to get myself some rest."

"Guess you don't want to go and play some cards later on tonight?" Lenny asked. "One of the guys from the site is dropping in to play."

"I should get some rest," Tony said. "But I might change my mind."

"Call me if you do."

"I'll do that." Tony turned the key in the ignition, then let the truck idle as he waved bye to Lenny. All he wanted to do was go home, beat off, then get some rest.

Driving home, Tony knew he had to find some way to get Vince out of his mind. He looked out at the highway stretching in front of him, and the other cars on either side. Traffic started slowing, so he pressed the clutch, then downshifted. His prick rubbed against his leg, which made his balls ache for release. He wasn't close to a rest area, or else he would stop and see if he could get some action. Placing his hand on his thick, bulging shaft, he told it they'd be home soon enough.

Then the traffic slowed even more. Moving his hand from his crotch to the steering wheel, Tony brought his foot down on the clutch one more time. His cock head started to throb, and he knew it was filling up with a load of hot nut juice. The traffic was moving slower, but at least it was moving. Up ahead was his exit, Route 10 Cranston. The large green sign was less than a mile away. He flicked his directional on to get into the right lane, peered at the red BMW and hoped the driver wouldn't decide to speed up and not let him through. The BMW paused. He was golden. Slowly, he turned the wheel and slid the truck into position.

Tony's right leg moved slightly, and his shaft gave him that tingly I-want-to-cum sensation again. It felt like his swollen cock head was full to the brim with spunk. Tony placed his hand on his shaft once more. The warmth of his hand felt good against his prick. He gave it a slow rub, easing his palm up close to the ripe head that was pinned beneath the denim. It felt good. He nearly let out a moan, but kept his composure. He couldn't let himself cream in the middle of traffic. He slid his hand down, then up again. If he didn't stop, he was going to blow his load.

Up ahead, the traffic only looked worse, with no end in sight. But his exit was close. He could make it. Still, his prick was begging for attention. He tried to ignore the pressure. Traffic slowed to a near stop. Tony had to press down on the clutch again. There it was, the rubbing of his cock head against denim and leg. He took a deep, sudden breath. His cock head pulsed. Tony's hand flew to his lap. It was too late, the first thick load had burst and wet his pant leg. He stroked his shaft through the denim as even more spunk shot out in pulsing bursts of hot jizm that covered his upper thigh.

By the time he was done creaming, the Route 10 Cranston exit was in front of him. Tony turned onto the on ramp, then headed home. He'd have to make sure to park in the garage so the neighbors wouldn't see the large cum stain.

At the construction site the next day, Tony found a shaded area to eat his lunch where nobody would find him. He'd spent most of the day working on the same level as Vince, and he couldn't keep his dick from showing itself any more. At one point he'd thought his hardon was going to rip through his jeans. The spot he'd found was behind a brick wall that hadn't been torn down near the rear of the property. The wall cast some shade, and helped his body cool down a bit from the day's exertion. If anyone dropped by and asked why he was spending his lunch alone, he'd just say he wanted to try and stay cool. Chances were good that nobody would even care, though.

Tony dropped his metal lunch box on the ground next to him, opened the rounded lid and pulled out the thick roast beef sandwich he'd made early that morning. Maybe if he was lucky he'd be able to scoff down the sandwich, then head off and stroke his prick. He really needed to do something before his balls started to ache. If Vince wasn't so fucking hot Tony wouldn't be in this mess. He couldn't help but check out Vince's ass every time he bent over. If Tony kept ending each day with a raging boner, the guys would tease him to no end.

There were footsteps. Tony paused mid chew to listen, hoping whoever it was would go away. Then he heard a voice.

"Hey there. Mind if I join you?" It was Vince, clutching a brown paper bag.

Tony moved his lunch box in front of himself, then motioned for Vince to sit next to him. Things were getting worse. He watched the bulge between Vince's legs shift with each step as he walked up to him. Vince paused near Tony, then slowly sat down.

"It's hot," Vince said, dropping his lunch bag on the ground to his right. He pulled his t-shirt over his head, took if off, then used it to wipe sweat from beneath his armpits. Vince's upper chest had a thick patch of hair that tapered off to a happy trail that disappeared inside his jeans. "Doesn't much matter, I'll be sweating in this t-shirt again once lunch is over."

"I know how you feel," Tony said, imagining how great it would be to kneel in front of Vince at the end of the day and suck his sweaty balls.

"I bet you do," Vince said, his eyes quickly darting towards Tony's crotch, then back up. "You can only take it for so long, then you have to do something about it. It's not like we work in air conditioning or anything."

"I hear you," Tony said, looking down at his sandwich and taking a bite. His cock was about to twitch from having Vince sitting so close. He could feel the guy's heat rising off his body.

"So, I hear you sometimes play cards with Lenny," Vince said.

"Sometimes. It's good to get out and spend time with guys you like," Tony said.

Vince scratched his balls. "I've played with him a few times. He really knows how to use his hand."

Tony told himself that Vince was referring to playing cards, and that it only sounded dirty because he was so fucking horny. "He's good at cards." Tony tried to concentrate on eating his sandwich, but it wasn't easy with Vince sitting next to him with no shirt on. He couldn't wait for lunch to be over.

It was the end of the day and Tony's balls were crying out for him to get off. He'd never had blue balls in his life, and if what he had now was any indication of what it was like, he would give to any charity looking for donations to eradicate it. Up ahead, Vince was leaning against the rear passenger side of his truck chatting with Lenny. The way the truck was sitting, it looked as if the rear driver's side wheel was resting in a hole.

Lenny shook Vince's hand, then walked off to his truck.

"Hey there," Vince called out, waving his hand at Tony. "I was talking to Lenny, and he's thinking of inviting a few of the boys over for a game of cards, you game?"

Tony wasn't sure if he'd be able to control himself playing cards all night and drinking beer with Vince sitting at the table. "I'm pretty busy this weekend," Tony said.

"That's fine, because we haven't set a date yet," Vince said.

Tony tried not to move too much to ease the rubbing of his jeans against his shaft. Looking around, Tony noticed that only his and Vince's trucks were left on the grounds. "Let me know when, and I'll join you guys," Tony said. Vince still had his dirty t-shirt on.

"We'll do that," Vince said.

Tony started walking towards his truck, thinking about what he wanted to do with Vince. Vince followed him around the back of the truck, then paused when he reached the driver's side.

"Shit!" Vince said.

Tony turned. "What's up?"

"I got a fucking flat tire," Vince said, giving the deflated tire a nudge with the toe of his yellow work boot. "Can you believe it?"

The site was far from any road, and the sun was going to start setting in an hour or so. Tony knew he should ask if he needed help, just to be polite. Vince probably would say no, anyhow. "You need a hand?"

"Sure, if you don't mind keeping me company," Vince said.

Now Tony was in trouble. "Not at all," Tony said, then he watched as Vince scooted under his truck and unhitched the spare tire. Tony told himself he'd be fine as long as Vince kept his shirt on. He looked away, not wanting Vince's exposed lower torso to start giving him any ideas.

"Nothing sucks more than getting a flat," Vince said, rolling the tire away from the truck, then letting it fall. He positioned the jack under the truck, just behind the flat tire, then started cranking it until the truck began to rise. When the flat tire was still touching the ground, Vince stopped. He peeled off his t-shirt, then tossed it into the back of the truck. "I won't be needing that."

"Want me to help loosen the nuts?" Tony asked, trying to keep himself from staring at Vince's nuts.

"That's okay," Vince said as he picked up the tire iron and set it in place. Leaning forward, his firm ass facing Tony, Vince let out a grunt, then loosened the first nut. He had three more to go.

Tony watched Vince's bottom, wondering how nice it would look outside of his jeans. And by the time Vince had finished loosening the nuts, Tony's balls were really aching to release their load.

"Want to roll that tire over here," Vince said as he went back to cranking the jack to raise the truck further off the ground.

Tony grabbed hold of the tire and rolled it over to where Vince was crouched down, removing each nut. Vince pulled the flat tire off the truck, then let it rest on the ground to his left. Turning, Vince placed a hand on Tony's leg, then looked up at him and grinned. Vince's face was at crotch level, and Tony's shaft gave a slight twitch.

"I need the tire," Vince said.

Tony rolled the tire out to him, then watched the muscles in Vince's back shift and stretch as he put the tire on, then replaced the nuts. Standing, Vince took a step back and brushed his back against Tony. Tony's hands went immediately to Vince's waist, feeling the hard muscle beneath smooth skin. Vince didn't move, nor could Tony take his hands off Vince. Instead, he slid his hands around the man's waist, feeling the firm stomach and thin line of hair that separated the two perfect halves of his chest.

Vince's head fell back onto Tony's shoulder, then turned. The two men kissed, their mouths opening to greet each others' tongues. Reaching between Vince's legs, Tony grabbed the bulging mass of man meat. Vince let out a sigh as Tony massaged the firm lump of cock and balls.

Finally, Tony was getting what he'd wanted. He had this handsome man in his grip. Tony rubbed his crotch against Vince's firm ass, wanting to go further, to undress him. He wanted to feel Vince's shaft in his grip and tug on the guy's nuts until he blew his load.

Vince turned, facing Tony, then lifted Tony's t-shirt up, over his head. Then he unbuttoned Tony's jeans. Reaching inside, he pulled out Tony's thick shaft, took it in his grip and gave it a stroke before going down on his knees.

Vince's lips stretched around Tony's prick, as his soft tongue caressed the underside of his rod. Tony closed his eyes, trying to hold back his load. It wasn't an easy job, especially the way Vince expertly swallowed every last inch of his meat. Finally he had to tell him to stop, that he was going to cum.

Looking up at him, Vince said, "I want to see that." He gave Tony's prick a squeeze.

"Not yet," Tony said. "Come up here."

Vince stood. Tony held his open palm against Vince's furry pecs, feeling the moist skin beneath. He pressed his thumbs against the nickel sized nipples, feeling the little nubs of flesh in the center of each. Then he ran his hands down the center of Vince's chest, tracing the thin trail of hair into his jeans. Slowly, he undid each button. Beneath the jeans was a pair of white briefs. Tony dipped his hand inside the briefs. When he pulled out Vince's shaft, the fleshy tube rose up a good six and a half inches, with a round, purple head that oozed precum. Reaching in again, he took out Vince's big hairy balls, which hung low between his legs. Tony wrapped his fingers around the stretched sack and gave Vince's nuts a gentle tug.

"Shit, that feels good," Vince said.

Tony pulled down again, then went on his knees. Vince's prick bobbed in front of Tony's face, the head staring at him and dripping precum. Tony licked around the head, then started sucking on the bulbous knob. Soon he felt Vince's hand on his head, pushing his mouth further onto his fuck stick. And Tony swallowed the full length in one gulp, then eased it out of his throat.

Tony's shaft wanted some attention, too, but Tony knew that if he touched his rod, it would shoot. He wanted to enjoy the time he had with Vince. He'd wanted to have this moment for so long, and had fought back his desire, thinking it would never come. He was going to make it last as long as he could.

Pulling Vince's dick out of his mouth, he leaned back and watched it drip with his excess spit. Vince's jeans were down around his ankles, and his big hairy legs were slightly separated.

"You really know how to give head," Vince said.

"Turn around, and let me show you something else," Tony said.

Vince turned, his firm, round ass inches from Tony's face. It looked so good that Tony leaned into it and bit the right cheek. Vince let out a gasp. "Be nice, man." Vince was going to see what nice was, Tony thought as he spread Vince's butt cheeks and dove in. The sweet smell of ass filled his nostrils like heady cologne. He licked along the sweaty crack, bringing his hands up to the small of Vince's back to get him to bend down. Tony wanted that pretty little pucker. He wanted to tickle it with the tip of his tongue and get it all wet with his spit.

Vince leaned forward, and Tony went to town. First he licked it with the flat of his tongue, then he moved back and parted Vince's ass further apart to get a good view of the tight little bud. There it was, winking hello. That was what he wanted.

"Come on, man, rim me," Vince said.

And Tony did. He tickled that tight fuck hole with his tongue, then poked his middle finger inside. He spit on the hole again, then stuck in another digit. Vince's ass lips kissed his fingers as he moved them in and out of the tight hole, finger fucking him.

"Your cock would feel a lot better," Vince said. "I have a condom in the truck."

"Get it," Tony said, then watched as Vince went to the truck and came back with a condom and a packet of lubricant. Tony unrolled the condom over his prick, then lubed it up as Vince got back into a squatting position. Reaching behind himself, Vince parted his cheeks to expose his pucker.

After slapping his cock head against Vince's hole, Tony slid the head inside. Vince's tight fuck ring gripped the head, then Tony gently eased his entire length deep inside Vince's bowels. Warmth engulfed his prick as he held it inside for a minute, then slowly pulled back. Vince's ass was so tight. He pulled back until the entire shaft was out of Vince's hole, then shoved it back in with one quick thrust.

"Oh man," Vince called out. "Fuck me."

That was Tony's cue. Gripping Vince's hips, Tony started pounding his prick in and out of his fuck hole. Vince wanted to get it up the ass, and Tony was going to give it to him. He rode Vince's ass good and hard, forcing his body to slam into Vince's ass.

It didn't take long before Tony felt his cock head about to burst. Tony pulled back one last time, then shot his first load of jizm on the thrust. He emptied more of his spunk with each inward glide, until he shot his entire load. Tony pulled his prick out of Vince's hole, then pulled off the condom and tossed it. Vince turned and stroked his shaft. Then his legs tightened, back arched, and he shot a load of hot spunk in the air, then another. With each shot of hot fuck juice, Vince's body jerked until his balls were emptied.

"That was real nice," Tony said.

Vince shook off the last drops of jizm. "Glad you liked it." Vince smiled. "You up for playing with me and Lenny some time?"

"Playing?" Tony asked.

"No, I don't mean cards," Vince said, then buttoned up his jeans and went back to work getting the tire secured to the truck. "Like I told you before, Lenny's real good with his hands."

Tony laughed. "I would love it, just let me know when."

BILLY'S DAD

It was a warm summer day, and the small white bathroom tiles weren't even cool beneath Joey's feet. Joey's jean shorts were bunched up around his ankles, and the black t-shirt with Korn scratched out in white across the front was on the floor in front of the sink. Joey separated his legs and let his big balls hang in the toilet bowl as he wrapped his fingers around his dick. His entire shaft, except for the head, was now in his grip. It felt good. He gently smoothed his hand over his narrow torso and wished he'd had thick, dark chest hair like Mr. Flood, his friend Billy's father.

Moving the soft pink curtains to the side, Joey leaned forward and watched Mr. Flood mow his lawn. Joey was safe as long as Mr. Flood didn't look up. And why would Mr. Flood look up at the second floor of his house? Mr. Flood's lawn mower roared as he leaned forward and pushed it with his strong, hairy arms. Sweat glistened on Mr. Flood's back, and his ass shifted in the dark blue shorts. Joey wished he'd turn the lawn mower around and show the dark curls of hair that covered his chest, not to mention the small belly that all men who have desk jobs seem to get. At least that was what Joey's father had always said was the reason for his little tummy when his mother complained about it.

Joey slowly moved his grip over his cock head, then down to his balls. He wished he could see Mr. Flood naked, maybe stepping out of the shower. But the bathroom in the Flood house was on the opposite side, so there was no way Joey would be able to see, even with a pair of binoculars. Leaning back, he imagined what Mr. Flood would look like naked. Judging from the size of the bulge he'd seen between Mr. Flood's legs, Joey assumed he was hung like a horse. He already knew Billy was hung. Not to mention uncut. If Joey could get close to Mr. Flood, he would suck his cock the same way he sucked Billy's. He'd peel back the foreskin and lick around the head, then slap his meat against his face a few times before taking the entire shaft down his eager throat. He'd even dive down and lick his asshole. He'd give anything to tickle Mr. Flood's pucker with his tongue.

"Joey, you asleep in there!" Joey's father called out from behind the door.

Joey let out a gasp as the first wave of hot cum spewed onto his stomach. He gulped air. "I'll be out in a minute, dad." The second shot hit his navel, then the third spilled out and over his fingers. Joey's father's heavy footsteps echoed down the hall. Moving his hand away from his dick, he licked the creamy froth off his fingers, then grabbed a wad of toilet paper from the roll and wiped up the sticky mess.

After this summer, Joey would be moving to college, and so would Billy. Who knew when Joey would get the chance to see Mr. Flood dressed only in sneakers and shorts again. Peering out the window, he watched as Mr. Flood stood full frontal and wiped sweat off his brow with the back of his hand.

If only Joey could find a way to suck that man's cock.

"Is Billy home, Mr. Flood?" Joey asked, trying not to look too longingly into Mr. Flood's deep brown eyes. Mr. Flood wore a pair of beige walking shorts and a simple green button down shirt. His big feet were bare.

"Come on in," Mr. Flood said, moving to the side. "He's in the shower, but you can wait for him in his room."

"Sure," Joey said, then walked up to the staircase. He paused at the railing and watched Mr. Flood pad across the hardwood floor and into the living room. "What are you doing tonight, Mr. Flood?"

Dropping onto the blue and white striped sofa, Mr. Flood pointed at the lap top computer on the mahogany coffee table. "Work, what else."

"Not looking at Internet smut, I hope," Joey said.

A grin spread over Mr. Flood's face, then he turned the computer around to show Joey the spread sheet full of names and numbers glowing on the screen. "I don't think I'll have time."

"It's a sad day, Mr. Flood," Joey said, then walked upstairs.

The shower was running as Joey walked past the bathroom door, then took a left to peek into Mr. Flood's bedroom. The bureau had framed pictures of Billy when he was young, one of which had him grinning with a bat held high over his left shoulder, and a red baseball cap. Other pictures were of Mr. Flood during his college days, standing in a park with some friends, all of whom looked young and athletic. A queen size bed with a simple wood frame was in the center of the room, the headboard pushed up against the wall. There wasn't a bedspread over it, just a set of white sheets tightly folded around the mattress. A pair of white briefs were under the bed. He'd probably missed them when he changed and put the dirty clothes in the hamper. That pair of briefs had to smell of Mr. Flood's balls and ass. Joey's cock started getting hard. He thought about sneaking in and taking a whiff. It was probably the closest he'd ever get to the real thing. Billy was in the shower, so he might have time. But the shower wasn't running.

"My bedroom is over there," Billy said, standing in the doorway to the bathroom with just a towel wrapped around the lower part of his smooth body. His dime sized nipples were hard, and there was a hint of an erection behind the towel.

"I was just being nosey," Joey said.

The two boys walked into Billy's bedroom, and Joey closed the door behind them. The bed hadn't been made, and the sheets were bunched at the footboard. To the left of the bureau was a pile of jeans and colored t-shirts. Billy dropped the towel on the floor, then fell back onto the bed and allowed the springs to bounce him.

"Why don't you join me?" Billy asked, patting the mattress to his left.

Joey kicked off his sandals and sat on the bed. Running his fingers through Billy's dark pubic hair, he wondered if Billy's father had the same type of dick. He grabbed Billy's semi-hard cock, feeling the weight of all six thick inches in his grasp. The cock head spilled a thin stream of precum onto Joey's fingers.

"Let me see your dick," Billy said.

"But what if your father comes in?" Joey asked. The mere thought made his cock stir.

"Nothing's going to bother him tonight," Billy said. "He's working on some new project or other."

Joey unbuttoned the fly of his shorts and pulled out his dick, which was hard and ready for action, then pulled off his shirt and tossed it to the side. "Why don't we just jerk each other off? We don't have a lot of time before the movie anyhow." He reached back and grabbed hold of Billy's shaft.

"We can come back and do more after the movie," Billy said, then took hold of Joey's prod and slowly started stroking him.

Closing his eyes, Joey leaned forward and gently kissed Billy on the lips. He imagined it was Billy's father he was kissing, and strok-ing. If only that were true, if only it was Billy's father's cock head plumping up with each upward stroke that caused his overhang to glide over the head and ooze yet more precum. Joey pulled away, then rolled onto his back. His body tightened and he shot his load.

"I don't care what anyone says, Keanu Reeves is hot," Billy said, steering the '92 VW Jetta into the driveway. The headlights of the car lit the garage door as Billy let the car idle.

"He's okay," Joey said. Someone a little older was more what Joey liked, although he did find Keanu handsome.

Billy lowered his eyebrows to show disapproval. "You wouldn't suck his dick if he asked?"

"You didn't ask that," Joey said, noticing that the lights were off at Billy's home. "Your dad's already asleep."

"Sure, midnight and he's in bed." Billy cut the engine, then rubbed Joey's leg. "You coming inside?"

"Is Keanu waiting inside?" Joey asked.

"No, but you can suck mine."

Both boys got out of the car, then headed for the house. At the front door, Billy fumbled with the key ring until he found the house key. Once the door was open, both boys stepped inside, then Billy slowly closed the door.

It was dark inside, but Joey had been in the Flood house enough times to know where he was going. He walked upstairs with Billy close behind until he reached the second floor landing. Mr. Flood's bedroom door was open. Taking a peek, Joey saw Mr. Flood's bare foot and calf. It looked as if Mr. Flood slept on his stomach.

"Come on," Billy whispered.

They stepped into Billy's room, then closed the door. Billy turned on the small lamp on the bedside table, which sent a dim light through the room. By the time Joey had his sandals and shirt off, Billy was already naked and lying on the bed pulling on his nuts. Joey pulled off his shorts, then his underwear. Climbing onto the bed, he tongued Billy's navel, then started to lick his way up for a kiss, but Billy's hand stopped him. Moving his head to the side, Joey got out of Billy's reach and looked up at him.

"Just suck my dick," Billy whispered.

"How sweet."

Billy let out a huff. "We can sixty-nine, if you want."

"Sure," Joey said. Once more, the condoms he'd brought weren't going to be used. Moving around, Joey wrapped his arm around Billy's waist and tucked his fingers in his ass crack. It didn't take much to get Billy's shaft in his mouth, just open mouth and lunge. After that he slid the entire length of Billy's shaft down his throat and held it there, feeling Billy do the same. Billy lifted his leg, making it easier for Joey's fingers to play with his tight hole. The little pucker was hot as Joey pushed his index finger against it, feeling it open and suck on the first section of the digit. Then Billy started moving his hips, gently sliding his fuck stick in and out of his mouth, massaging his throat. Closing his eyes, Joey imagined that it was Billy's dad that was fucking his face while sucking his cock.

Joey concentrated on the mouth around his prick. The moist heat drove him wild, making his prick fill with hot jizm. Joey pulled his prick out of Billy's mouth, then felt a hand grip his shaft and stroke it.

Taking the cock out of his mouth, Joey grabbed hold of the fleshy tube and stroked it in time with the hand jerking his own prick. Mr. Flood, he thought.

Billy let out a groan. Joey didn't move his face away from the ripe head playing peek-a-boo in his grip. There was another groan, then Billy's body jerked, and a hot blast of cum hit Joey's face, then another landed on his chin. Rolling onto his back, Joey let the final bursts of jizm spray his neck. Then Joey's spunk spewed out of his own piss slit and coated his stomach.

"Shit, that was good." Billy leaned over the edge of the bed, his round ass facing up, then tossed a towel at Joey. "Clean yourself up." Billy sat up with his legs crossed. "You're covered in the stuff."

The towel was somewhat stiff near one edge, so Joey used the opposite end to wipe off his face before the creamy white juice dripped onto the bed. "Maybe I should just rub it in and see if it really does make a good facial."

"You're fucking gross sometimes, you know that," Billy said.

Joey wiped off his stomach. "Have a sense of humor."

"You crashing here tonight?"

Joey stood up, then searched the floor for his clothes. "I just want to take a shower and snooze." He got dressed as Billy slid under the covers. "I'll be quiet walking out."

"Cool."

Once dressed, Joey held onto his sandals and walked out of Billy's room, making sure to close the door with little noise. Mr. Flood's bedroom was only two feet away. He snuck over and peered inside. The bed was empty. The bathroom door was open. Mr. Flood had to be downstairs. Hopefully he would not run into him on his way out. And what if he did run into him, what would happen then? Nothing. Joey walked to the top of the stairs. He wondered if Mr. Flood walked around the house naked. It was late at night, and he didn't know that Billy had had company. Joey's best bet was to not run into Mr. Flood, that way he wouldn't accidentally do or say anything stupid. How would he explain why he was there so late? He couldn't tell the truth.

One by one, Joey took each step, hoping there wouldn't be a creak or a telltale sound to announce his presence. When he reached the bottom of the stairs, he peered to the left, into the living room. His heart nearly stopped beating when he saw Mr. Flood sitting on the sofa, leaning forward as he finished the final bite of a sandwich. Mr. Flood's green robe was open, and his cock was rock hard, jutting up between his legs. Joey stood perfectly still, not wanting to make his presence known, and wanting to see as much of Mr. Flood's naked body as he could. Joey's cock was getting hard again, and making itself noticeable by forming a bulge in his shorts.

Then Mr. Flood saw Joey, covered himself, and stood up, his hard cock making the robe tent out a little. Fighting the urge to bolt out the door, Joey waved and mouthed hello. He walked into the living room. "I was just leaving," he whispered.

Mr. Flood smiled. "How was the movie?" Mr. Flood took a seat, then patted the space to his left.

"Awesome," Joey said, sitting down. The lap top computer was still on the coffee table, turned off. "You worked all night?"

"Afraid so." Mr. Flood's brown eyes looked straight into Joey's. "I don't have much choice."

"That must suck." Joey couldn't help but notice that Mr. Flood's robe was open enough to show the dark curly hairs that covered his chest. "Don't you get lonely?" Joey shifted to give his shaft room to grow.

"Sometimes." Mr. Flood sighed. "But I don't want to date, and I don't want to put Billy through having to meet anyone new."

"I don't think he would care."

Mr. Flood raised his eyebrows. "Oh, I'm not too sure about that." He opened his legs and the front of the robe parted, exposing nothing but the deep green material of the robe underneath. His large cock twitched beneath the material, and rose up higher. "Not to mention that I'm an old man now."

"No you're not," Joey said, giving Mr. Flood's knee a pat, which was enough to cause the robe to slide off to the side and expose his leg. "You're still a good looking man."

"That's nice to hear," Mr. Flood said, planting his big hand on Joey's left shoulder. Joey glanced down before their eyes met once more. "You shouldn't have a problem finding anyone." Joey's voice was slightly shaky. He forced a grin, then looked up at Mr. Flood. Mr. Flood's hand moved around to the back of Joey's head, his fingers sliding through the hair at the nape of his neck.

Placing his hand on Mr. Flood's knee, Joey slid it up his hairy thigh, between the fold in the robe. Mr. Flood's big hairy balls were in his reach. Joey grabbed them, then felt Mr. Flood lead his head down onto his lap.

Joey parted the robe, exposing the six inch staff rising up from the cloth, the beautiful full head half covered by foreskin. Gripping the thick rod, Joey pulled down, causing the fleshy hood to move away from the swollen knob.

"Suck it," Mr. Flood whispered.

Joey sucked the entire prick down his throat, then started to ease his lips up and down the shaft. Mr. Flood sighed and let out soft groans. It didn't take long before the head grew plump and ready to spew.

"Stop," Mr. Flood whispered.

Joey slid the cock out of his mouth, then wiped spit off his lips with the palm of his hand. He was in trouble. Mr. Flood must have felt a tinge of guilt about having his son's best friend blow him. Joey didn't know what to say, but felt he had to do or say something before his fantasy was ruined.

"I want to fuck you," Mr. Flood said.

Joey choked back a laugh. Pushing his hand into the right pocket of his shorts, he fished out the condom and held it up like a trophy.

"We're golden."

Joey dropped his drawers and pulled off his t-shirt. He unrolled the lubricated condom over Mr. Flood's dick, then planted each foot on either side of Mr. Flood's body and sat down until he felt the domed tip of his dick against his pucker. Joey lowered himself down on Mr. Flood's shaft, feeling it stretch his fuck hole wider than it had ever been stretched before. When he was half way down, he stopped. Mr. Flood wrapped his arms around Joey, pulling him close.

"Go slow," Mr. Flood whispered.

Joey took a deep breath, then slowly released it as he continued to sit on the massive shaft. Once it was buried deep in Joey's ass, Mr. Flood slipped his hands under Joey's ass, and helped him glide up and down his pole. The hair on Mr. Flood's belly tickled Joey's balls as he rode him. Mr. Flood's hot breath slapped his neck in a steady beat.

Joey grabbed his swollen shaft and gave it a few strokes. But he didn't want to cum until Mr. Flood squirted up his butt, so he stopped.

"Get on your back," Mr. Flood said, then wrapped his big arms around Joey's waist and held him as he shifted on the sofa.

Joey gripped Mr. Flood's shoulders, their warm bodies close together. Mr. Flood stood, then walked to the middle of the room and gently lowered Joey onto the floor without pulling his cock out of his ass. Once on the floor, with the rug against his back, Joey lifted his legs and Mr. Flood started easing his massive prick in and out of his fuck hole. Mr. Flood grabbed hold of Joey's ankles, then slammed his fleshy tube back and forth with more force than before.

Joey couldn't believe how good it felt to have Billy's daddy fucking his ass. His cock was rock hard, the head ripe once more. And Mr. Flood's cock head was already plumping up in his bowels, getting ready to burst.

"I'm going to cum," Mr. Flood whispered.

Joey grabbed his dick and gave it a few strokes, then felt a quick jab as Mr. Flood's cock started to twitch, and the head throbbed. Mr. Flood was coming up his ass. Joey gave his shaft a few more strokes, then let out a gasp. The first of his jizm squirted onto his upper chest, then the rest splattered on his stomach in bursts of thick, frothy fuck juice.

Mr. Flood pulled his meat out of Joey's pucker. Joey felt his hole shrinking back to normal, then sat up. "I need something so I can clean up," he whispered.

"Stay there," Mr. Flood said, then padded out of the room. He came back with a paper towel, and used it to wipe the thick white spunk off Joey's torso. When he was finished, he gave Joey a gentle kiss on the lips. "You made my night. It's been so long since I've done anything like that."

"Maybe you should tell Billy," Joey said. "Not about us, but about you."

Mr. Flood grinned and nodded. "You won't tell him about this. I mean, he wouldn't be too happy to hear that I fucked his best friend."

"This is between us." Joey started collecting his clothes.

Mr. Flood slipped back into his robe, not bothering to tie the sash. "You don't think he'll mind having a gay father?"

"No," Joey said, "I don't think he'll mind at all."

JAY'S FRIEND

This all would have never happened if I hadn't become roommates with a straight guy. I was just out of college, working an entry level job that paid next to nothing after taxes, and needed a decent place to live. My choices were living in a dump or living with a roommate in a decent place. Finding a roommate was my best bet, so I hunted through the papers and found a place with a straight guy named Jay. Jay was tall and thin, with strawberry blond hair and gray blue eyes. He had a penchant for wearing baggy clothes, and a habit of leaving his porn mags lying around the apartment. And, on top of that, he kept an issue of Jugs in a drawer under the bathroom sink.

The apartment was spacious, and had hardwood floors and eggshell walls. A dull green overstuffed sofa sat against the wall in front of a set of windows that overlooked downtown Providence. The jade oriental rug on the floor was in need of cleaning, and the corner nearest the front door was slightly curled. The kitchen was eat-in, and the table sat four comfortably. At the far end of the kitchen was the bathroom. Green tiles lined the bathroom floor, and ran halfway up the walls. Living on a hill gave us a wonderful view of the small cluster of buildings rising up from downtown. The apartment was perfect for viewing the fireworks on the Fourth of July, and was just a stone's throw away from Waterfire, an evening event where small fires are lit on pillars set evenly apart in the Providence River.

Jay was cool about my living with him. He didn't pry into my life, stayed with his girlfriend a few nights a week, and didn't expect anything of me except my half of the rent and utilities. Everything was going well, and I was afraid of coming out to him and having him get all weird on me. And because of that I got into the habit of not taking men back to my place, but always going to their apartments.

I was able to hide the slight dysfunction of my living arrangements until I met this hot go-go boy at Mirabar one Friday night. The go-go boy's name was Todd, and he was smooth and dark, with muscles that rippled under his skin like gentle waves on the ocean. We talked for a bit, and I explained that I was living with a straight boy and didn't bring guys home. Todd laughed, then brought me to his small, one bedroom apartment for some fun.

Todd closed his apartment door, then walked me into his bedroom. "How long have you been living with a straight boy?" he asked.

"Two weeks," I said.

"And how long before you move out?" he asked while unbuttoning his baby blue shirt, exposing his smooth chest.

I reached out and placed my hands against Todd's youthful skin, sliding them around his waist. "I don't know," I said. "It might work out in the end."

"Not unless you tell him." Todd turned to me and pressed his full lips against mine. His tongue poked inside my mouth, running over my teeth. Our lips parted, and I went to the floor and unbuttoned his baggy pants, let them fall to his ankles, then pulled down on the elastic waist band of his boxer shorts. His dark pubic hair showed, then his long, thin cock sprung out in front of my face. The head was shielded by foreskin that rose up over the swollen knob. Pulling the foreskin back, I exposed the rosy crown, then sucked it into my mouth.

He grabbed my head and eased his prick down my throat, then out until the head was on the tip of my tongue, then he slid his rod down my gullet once more. He pumped his cock in and out of my mouth a few more times before he pulled it out. I stood, and we both undressed completely. Our hands caressed each others' bodies, roaming over smooth flesh. Then I was on the floor, my chest and legs pressed against the deep pile carpet as he licked my ass, then probed my tight pucker with his fingers. After slipping on a condom, he shoved his cock up my ass and gave me a good, hard fuck until he blew his load.

I turned onto my back and he grabbed my prick tight, gently kissed me full on the mouth, then stroked my shaft. It didn't take long before I felt my fleshy tube fill with hot spunk. Then my legs tightened, and I blew my frothy load all over my stomach and chest.

The next two weeks all I could think about was Todd telling me that I had to come out to my roommate, so I threw myself into my job in a lame attempt to forget about it. I worked until eight o'clock at night, then went home and made something quick to eat. Jay was usually hanging around the apartment in rumpled clothes, reading the paper with his feet up on the coffee table, or watching some television program. I know it sounds silly that I was afraid to tell Jay about myself, but I could not imagine a man who read Jugs would be cool about living with a gay guy.

Then late one Sunday night everything changed. I had just come back from watching a film at the Avon Cinema on Thayer Street and Jay was talking on the telephone in the kitchen. Although I tried not to listen to his conversation, a bit of it did reach my ears. Mostly when he said, "No, stay here. It shouldn't be a problem," and, "You'll like him," then, "I'm not sure, but I think so."

I kicked off my loafers, sat on the chair to the right of the sofa, then waited for Jay to get off the phone. If he was going to ask me something, I was going to be available. I heard the telephone hang up, then Jay hesitantly stepped into the living room. He gave me a nervous grin, then wiped his hands on his gray t-shirt. "Hey there," he said. "A friend of mine from New York is planning on moving to Providence. He'll be here for a couple of days to find an apartment before he starts his new job. Cash is kind of tight for him, so he was wondering if he can crash here for a few days. Would you mind?"

Not wanting to be an asshole, I had no choice but to say it was okay.

"He's coming in Thursday night. It's only until Sunday, then he goes back to New York until it's time for him to move," Jay said, then went back into the kitchen to call his friend and tell him to drop by.

And this is where the trouble for me begins. Jay's college pal was tall, muscular, and had an ass that filled out his chinos to their fullest potential. His dark hair was cropped short, and his well chiseled face begged to be kissed. It was difficult to keep my eyes away from his tight, ribbed pullover shirt that showed each ripple of muscle as he placed his brown leather suitcase on the floor.

"This is Michael," Jay said.

Michael held out his hand, and his big, thick fingers wrapped around my hand for a firm shake. My cock began to stir, and I had to make an effort not to drool.

"I hope this doesn't inconvenience you any," Michael said, his voice deep and masculine. "I'll start looking for a place first thing in the morning."

Then Jay invited me to play some cards with them, so I agreed. We played a game of hearts and got to talking. I found out that Michael played baseball for a local team called Hawks, and knew everything imaginable about the stock market. I felt like the odd man out, but tried to appear interested in everything they talked about. If nothing else, I think it helped my game. After all, I did win.

After the card game, Michael stripped down to his blue plaid boxer shorts. Try as I might, I couldn't help but take notice of Michael's well defined pectorals dusted with dark hair that formed a thin line that separated his six pack and disappeared inside the elastic waistband of his shorts. His bulging meat bobbed and swayed in their loose cotton confines as he walked into the bathroom to brush his teeth. I went into my bedroom and shut the door for fear that my enjoyment of seeing Michael's naked torso and hefty basket was becoming too evident.

I undressed, then turned off the light and crawled into bed. Images of Michael in the next room entered my mind, and I couldn't get them out. I kept telling myself that the handsome, dark haired man sleeping on the sofa was straight, and that I could not jeopardize my cheap living situation by making a move on him, then turned onto my side and tried to sleep. But my stiff dick wouldn't let me forget about Michael. I turned onto my stomach, then shoved my hands beneath my pillow. Images of Michael's naked body resurfaced. All I could think about was how nice it would be to lie on top of Michael; to feel his soft flesh against my cock. I started humping the bed while thinking about rubbing myself against Michael's firm stomach and kissing him. And his ass was perfect, round and biteable. I wanted to go down on my knees and lick the crack, then tickle his pucker with my tongue.

Then my cock twitched, and I shot my load on the sheets.

I woke up late the next morning, and had to rush around to get ready for work. The bathroom door was closed, and the water in the sink was running. With a towel wrapped around my waist, I knocked on the door. "Are you going to be much longer, I'm running late," I said.

The door opened, and there was Michael, naked, standing in front of the sink with the end of a blue toothbrush sticking out of his frothy mouth. He stepped back, and I had to make an effort to keep my eyes from glancing down at his thick, uncut shaft and low hanging balls. He pulled the toothbrush out of his mouth, then spit white froth into the sink. "Go ahead," he said. "I'm almost done."

So I stepped past him, making sure the front of my towel didn't brush up against his perfect ass. Michael washed the remainder of the toothpaste from his mouth as I got the shower water to a comfortable temperature.

Michael turned, leaned against the sink and crossed his arms. His hairy balls hung loose between his legs, and his soft cock drooped down and to the right. "I really hope my being here isn't an inconvenience to you," he said.

"Not at all," I said, then dropped my towel while keeping my back to him. The last thing I wanted Michael to see was my raging hardon. I quickly stepped into the shower, grabbed the soap, then proceeded to lather my balls.

"Wish me luck looking for a new place," Michael said.

I wished him luck, then grabbed hold of my shaft and gave it a stroke.

"Do you want the door closed?" Michael asked.

"No, open is fine," I said, then shot my load.

After work the same day I slipped into shorts and a t-shirt, then relaxed on the sofa with a good book. I'd read about twenty or so pages when Michael walked in, then slipped off his leather bomber jacket and dropped it on the edge of the sofa. His gray slacks still appeared freshly pressed.

"How was your day?" Michael asked.

"It was okay," I said.

Michael unbuttoned his white shirt, slipped it off, then tossed it on the chair to my left. I hoped his white t-shirt was next, but he sat down on the sofa and kicked off his patent leather shoes instead. "Thankfully I found a place on Medway Street. Apartment hunting can be a pain in the ass," he said, then kicked his socked feet on the coffee table. "Jay called me and said he had a date tonight, so I guess we're on our own."

A night alone with Michael! My cock started to rise, so I quickly stuffed my hands in my pants pockets.

"How about ordering a pizza and having a couple of beers," Michael said. "We can have a night with just the boys."

"Sounds like a plan," I said, hoping not to sound like a dork. "Why don't I call? What do you want on it?"

"Anything," Michael said, then stood up and pulled off his t-shirt. "I'm going to hop in the shower." Michael unbuttoned his slacks and let them fall to the floor. He stretched, and I saw the outline of his prick against the orange cotton boxer shorts.

"Why don't I make that call?" I said, then walked into the kitchen to use the telephone before Michael took anything else off.

I pulled the telephone book out of the drawer to the right of the kitchen sink, then dropped it on the table and started flipping the pages until I found the Pizza listings. My prick was rock hard, and forming a noticeable bulge between my legs.

"Hey, do you have a towel I can use?" Michael asked.

I turned, and there was Michael, naked, his semi-hard cock pointing out a good six inches in my direction, the foreskin bunched up around the swollen crown. I looked into his deep brown eyes and tried to tell myself that nothing was going to happen. "Let me get you one," I said, then walked into my bedroom with Michael not far behind. I opened my bedroom closet, then grabbed one of the thick purple terrycloth towels from the top shelf and tossed it at him.

Michael draped the towel over his left shoulder, then smiled. His eyes went down to my bulging crotch, then back to meet my gaze. "Why don't you join me," Michael said, not trying to conceal his hardening shaft.

I couldn't believe what I was hearing. "Join you?"

"Get naked," Michael said. "It's just us boys tonight." He reached forward, pressed his palm against my basket, then gave my meat a squeeze.

I gripped his prick, feeling the warm, stiff tube of flesh. Michael's tongue gently caressed my lips. He unzipped my pants, then slid his hand inside and pulled out my meat. Then he wrapped his fingers around my rod. I stepped back, then went down on my knees. Michael placed his hands on my head and eased his cock past my lips.

In one smooth glide I swallowed Michael's cock. His balls rested against my chin for a while, then he slowly eased his prick out of my mouth. When only the knob of his cock was against my lips, Michael began to ease his meat back down my gullet. His balls gently pushed against my chin with each inward glide of his hips as he fucked my mouth nice and slow.

My own cock was rock hard now, and I wanted more action than giving head, so I pulled his prick out of my mouth and started licking under his hairy sack. Michael separated his legs and squatted. I grabbed his balls, wrapping my fingers around the loose sack, pulling it up to expose the thin cord of flesh that ran from his nuts to his asshole. I ran my tongue along the cord, then placed my free hand on his ass so my thumb was pressed against his tight pucker. Michael's ass moved closer to my face. I stopped what I was doing and slid out from under him.

"What's up?" Michael asked.

I stood up, wrapped my arms around his waist and pressed my fingertips into his ass crack. "I want this," I said, tapping my middle finger against his fuck hole.

"Get a condom," Michael said.

I stepped back and walked to the bureau where I had some condoms stashed away in the top drawer. When I turned back around, Michael was lying on the bed with his hands behind his head and his legs stretched out. I couldn't believe I had this man on my bed, waiting for me to fuck him.

"What are you waiting for?" Michael said, then lifted his legs and grabbed his ankles, exposing his asshole.

I unrolled the condom over my prick, then knelt down on the bed and leaned close to his hole. The musky scent of his sweaty ass filled my nostrils as his pucker winked at me. I gave the hole a lick, then pressed both index fingers against it.

"Oh man, I like that," Michael said, his voice a soft whisper.

I spit on his hole, then pushed the first knuckle of each finger inside. Michael shifted his ass back and forth and let out a sigh. I stuffed more of my fingers into his ass.

"Come on, put your cock inside," Michael said.

Eager to please, I lubed Michael's ass up good, then pressed my knob against it and pushed. His ass ring opened to my cock head, then grabbed my shaft good and tight as it slowly eased up his fuck canal until the entire length of my prick was buried deep inside Michael's bowels. Then I grabbed Michael's ankles and gently pulled out until only the head was inside. I paused, then slid my rod back up his hot, smooth ass.

Michael's cock was still rock hard as he spit in his hand and grabbed his meat. I lifted his legs higher so Michael's swollen knob was inches from his beautiful mouth. Our eyes met when I paused mid fuck. Michael's ass ring clenched around my dick, then he stuck out his tongue and licked the drop of precum off his piss slit.

"Give it to me, man," Michael said as he stroked his cock.

I started slamming my fuck stick in and out of his tight ass. Michael let out a few soft groans as he continued to stroke his shaft. His cock head was only an inch or two from his open mouth, and I wanted to see him eat his own load.

Hot spunk started building up in my shaft, getting ready to shoot. Michael licked his lips, then opened his mouth. A thick glob of juicy jizz shot from his piss slit and landed on his tongue. That was all I needed to see to get my own cock shooting its frothy load. I pulled back, then slammed my fuck stick in deep. Another glob of spunk spewed from Michael's shaft and landed on his tongue. The next load of ball juice hit his lips, and the next hit his chin.

The last drips of my own spunk spilled out of my dick as Michael's jizz dripped from his piss slit and pooled up on his dark pubic hair. I pulled my cock out of his ass, then sat on the edge of the bed and peeled the cum filled condom off my prick.

Michael stretched, then sat up as I tossed the used rubber in the trash can next to the bed. "Well, now I guess Jay was right about you," he said.

"What do you mean?" I asked.

"He thought we'd be compatible, and we were."

I felt like such a fool. "You mean he knew all this time that I'm gay?"

"Suspected," Michael said, flashing his pearly whites.

I stood, then put my hands on my hips. "So this was a test? He couldn't just come out and ask?"

"You could have told him; it's not like all straight guys are homophobes."

Michael was right, I had prejudged Jay, although I hated to

admit it.

Michael raised his eyebrows, then said, "Maybe you can come visit me at my new place once I get settled in."

"When will that be?" I asked.

"Not for another two weeks," Michael said. "But, if you want to come to New York this weekend, you can stay with me."

Now there was an offer I could not refuse.

MYSTERY MAN

Tony pulled the bright yellow t-shirt over his head, then used it to wipe the beads of sweat off his brow. Leaning against the oak highboy, he looked at the freshly made queen size slay bed, then let out a sigh. All moved in, he thought. Finally. He'd spent the day unpacking and now he would be able to relax. He swiped the t-shirt over his firm pectorals, then his hard abdomen. He'd skip the gym; getting all his furniture moved into the bungalow had been workout enough for one day. The sneakers he wore were old, and battered, so he didn't bother unlacing them before pulling them off and kicking them under the bed. His gray cotton shorts were next to come off, but first he wanted to close the front door. He stepped out of the bedroom, into the hall, at the end of which was the bathroom. The spare bedroom was to the right, and across from that the opening that led to the kitchen and living room.

At the age of thirty he was finally able to buy his first home, and in a decent area. It was a bungalow, or so the real estate agent had told him. Tony didn't mind, he liked the idea of owning a small bungalow on the East Side of Providence. He padded into the living room, looked at how well his furniture fit. The forest green overstuffed sofa against one wall, his television across the room from the sofa. He'd been able to fit two bookshelves against the wall across from the bay windows at the front of the house. He stepped into the small mud room, then closed and locked the front door.

Tony turned towards the living room. He needed to get an area rug for the living room. The hardwood floors were beautiful, but he didn't like the slight discoloration in the middle of the floor. Nobody had even noticed the stain when he'd shown his friends the place before moving in. But he knew it was there. It was the spot where the body of the previous owner had been found two years ago, stabbed eight times in the back by a crazed drug addict. That was why the house had been so cheap, and he knew it. He'd even sought out the house knowing nobody would want it.

Peter had laughed when he'd told him about the house, and why he knew he could get it for a song. "You're so conniving," Peter had said. Tony crossed his arms, then leaned against the wall. Peter's comment about him had stung. If Tony was so conniving then why had it been Peter who had ended their five year relationship to be with a boy of twenty-two? Peter was thirty-nine; didn't he know how silly he looked hanging out with a bunch of young kids? Tony blinked the dampness from his eyes. Even three months after their break-up it still hurt.

It was getting dark; Tony would have to go and buy the rug tomorrow. What he wanted to do now was take a shower and try to forget about everything. He didn't feel like going out to a club for fear of running into Peter, but wanted to do something. Waterfire was going on downtown, and he thought he'd like to go to that. He could get lost in the crowd, maybe grab a bite to eat and relax near the Providence River. It was supposed to be a warm evening, and it would be a shame for him to stay inside.

Tony stepped into the small bathroom, then slipped out of his shorts. The white tiles were cool against his feet, and he leaned over the porcelain bathtub to pull the forest green shower curtain closed around the tub before turning on the shower. He stepped inside and felt the hot spray hit his back, loosening his stiff muscles. Leaning back, he felt water rush through his short hair, and pass over his torso. He ran his hands over his head, then turned to face the spray. Grabbing the bar of soap, he began to lather his big, hairy balls, then ran his hand over his stiffening shaft. He hadn't been laid since the break-up, and now he was feeling the need to have a naked man by his side. Reaching back, he ran the soap through the crack of his rounded ass cheeks, then placed the bar back in the soap dish set into the wall. He fingered his sudsy pucker, dipping his middle finger inside the tight hole and moving it in and out. If only he had someone with him to finger his hole.

With his free hand, Tony grabbed his stiff, uncut dick and gave it a few strokes. Then he took his finger out of his ass and straightened, feeling the spray against his chest and mist on his face. He slid his fist over this thick shaft. Hot cum started collecting at the swollen head, getting ready to burst. He tilted his head back, then felt his knees give slightly. He let out a soft groan, and the first shot of jizm spewed from his piss slit and slapped against the white tiled wall. Then the second shot rang out. He let out another moan. His balls continued to release their spunk with each successive stroke until they were empty.

A faint groan echoed from the bathroom. Tony peeled back the shower curtain and peered into the misty bathroom. "Hello?" he said.

Silence.

"Hello?"

Tony closed the shower curtain. It had probably been just his voice echoing, or a noise from outside.

Tony stood on the poured cement walkway over the river and watched the fires set in the braziers in the center of the waterway. To his left was downtown Providence, and above, the night sky and the full moon. Groups of people milled about on either side of the river, watching the fires, leaning over the thick, metal railing, sitting on the poured cement steps that led to the river. The flaming braziers went further down the river, set apart at equal distances. Tony crossed the bridge, then walked down the street, past a small group of people gathered together to watch a mime perform. The air was filled with the sound of crackling wood and the Gregorian Chants being fed from speakers overhead. Tony stuffed his hands in the pockets of his green walking shorts, then rubbed the toes of his right foot against the sole of his Birkenstock sandal. He slipped his foot back into the sandal, then walked down the steps, and made his way with the crowd following the river along its path.

The walkway led under a street bridge, where voices echoed and made the Gregorian Chant even more evocative. A small black barge with a group of four people dressed in black slowly made its way down the river to feed the fires set in the braziers. Tony leaned against the railing, listened to the sounds of the night, and inhaled the sweet scent of burning wood. Then Tony felt someone behind him, close to him. Hot breath hit the back of his neck, then he felt hands slipping under his shirt.

"Be still," a deep, male voice whispered. Then he felt the man's hips press against his ass, and his stiff cock pushing against him.

Voices echoed behind him, the chanting continued. The dark barge slowly drifted away. The man's thick fingers unbuttoned Tony's shorts, then unzipped his fly. Tony closed his eyes as the man lugged out his six stiff inches of uncut cock. Glancing downstream, Tony couldn't see another boat, just the fires burning around the slight bend. As the man began to slowly stroke Tony's shaft, his free hand slid beneath his shirt and caressed his smooth chest. The skin of Tony's prick rose up and down with the man's grip. The foreskin rose over the head, then went back down, and over again, bringing Tony closer to orgasm.

Tony hoped they wouldn't get caught. But it was dark under the bridge; nobody could see them. The man quickened his strokes. Tony's knees bent slightly, and he tightened his grip on the metal railing. Footsteps echoed behind him. The Gregorian chanting continued. The man gently pinched Tony's left nipple. Wood crackled and burned. The head of Tony's cock swelled. Tony bit his lower lip as the man's fist rose up over his cock head, then back down.

The man's hand circled Tony's swollen cock head, then rode down his rod, only to lift back up over the head. Tony stifled a groan. His knees buckled again, and he pressed his hands against the railing to keep from falling. He was close to coming. Tony took in a deep breath as the first wave of hot spunk shot into the night, rippling the water below. The man's fist continued to stroke Tony's rod as he continued to unload his spunk into the river until his balls were empty.

The man let go of Tony's shaft, then stepped back, leaving Tony to tuck himself into his shorts. He turned to see the man who had jerked him off, but couldn't see anyone in the crowd who was responsive to his stare. Was the man watching him, or had he run off? Tony didn't know.

Tony shifted into the crowd and walked out from under the bridge. Did the man know him? He tried to place the voice, but couldn't. It had to have been someone who knew him. Why would a stranger jerk him off in public? And why him? Tony turned, then stepped up the cement stairs that led to the street. The large, brick colonial Rhode Island School of Design auditorium was in front of him. He walked past the building, towards College Hill. The bus tunnel that was set into College Hill loomed in front of him like a black hole. Tony looked back. People continued on their way along the street. The music continued to play. The fires burned.

Halfway up College Hill, at the corner of Waterman and Benefit Streets, resting amongst a patch of lush green where students lounged on sunny days reading or chatting with friends, was a modern sculpture of curves in the center of the green. Tony stopped to look at the sculpture, then turned right onto Benefit Street, with its old, colonial houses and faux gas street lamps. He'd parked his car across from the RISD Museum. Tony walked along the red brick sidewalk and headed towards his car when he saw a man bending over, his hands cupping the water coming from a small fountain set into the side of a cement wall. The man wore jeans and a blue plaid shirt that hung open. He was Tony's size, and had short dark hair and pale skin. Standing up, the man turned towards Tony. The man's full lips glistened in the glow of the street lamp. Their eyes met, then a car horn honked, causing Tony to jump, then look behind him. A white VW Jetta drove past Tony, then an old Ford Escort hatchback.

When Tony turned back towards the fountain, the man was gone.

Tony slept, dreaming that he was home in bed. The man he'd seen on the street drinking from the fountain stood next to the bed, his stiff prick rising up six inches, and his low hanging balls dangling beneath. Slowly, the man crawled onto the bed, then slid the sheets off Tony's naked body. The man's hands were cool as they caressed Tony's chest, gliding down towards his bush of pubic hair. The man kissed Tony's chest, then ran his tongue down the center, past Tony's firm abdomen, over the hooded tip of his stiff dick, along the shaft, then stopped at his nuts. The man moved down between Tony's legs, then grabbed hold of Tony's rod and started stroking it as he sucked his balls into his mouth.

Tony's back arched, his legs parted, his toes curled. He let out a groan, then shot his creamy load onto his stomach.

The cement floor of the basement was cool against Tony's bare feet. There were a few boxes left from the man who had been murdered in the house. The basement was empty except for three 14 × 14 × 14 boxes that had been pushed to the corner, the flaps folded closed. Tony pressed the cordless telephone between his shoulder and jaw line as he sat on the floor, feeling the cool dampness seep through his seersucker shorts.

"I had the most wild wet dream last night," Tony said.

"Really." Gary sounded eager to hear more. "I haven't had one of those since college."

"Yes, it was a wonderful dream!" Tony said, then let out a slight shiver.

"What was that about?" Gary asked.

"I'm in the basement," Tony said. "It's kind of chilly."

"You're in the basement alone?" Gary said.

"You're such a pansy." Tony sat on the cool floor and pulled the first of the three boxes towards him. The box was light.

"What are you doing down there?" Gary asked.

"I'm curious about some boxes that were left behind," Tony said. "It's probably just holiday crap that nobody wanted."

"That or another dead body."

"They're just standard boxes, hardly big enough to hold a dead body," Tony said.

"Unless it was chopped into pieces."

Tony rolled his eyes, then opened the flap. He pushed his hand into the white Styrofoam kernels. Nothing.

"I can't believe you're opening that box," Gary said, a tinge of nerves present in his voice.

"Some very scary Styrofoam," Tony said, then pushed the box to his left and reached for the next, which was just as light as the previous one. He opened it to find more Styrofoam. "More of the same in the second."

"You're giving me the creeps," Gary said. "How can you be there alone?"

"It's just an empty basement." Tony reached out and pulled the last box away from the wall. It, too, was light. He was about to open the flaps when he noticed a photograph on the floor where the box had been. Tony leaned forward, getting on his knees, then picked up the photograph. "I found something," he said.

"What?"

"A picture." He looked at the picture of a naked man relaxing on a black leather sofa. The man's cock was soft, drooping to the left, the head almost touching the sofa cushion. It had to be six inches easy. His hairy balls hung low to his side. His torso was smooth and well formed, his hair was dark, and cut short. His lips were full.

"Tony?"

"I'm here," Tony said, staring at the photograph. The man looked familiar. "Can I call you back?"

"Sure," Gary said. "Is everything okay?"

"Yes, it's fine. Just let me call you back." Tony slipped the phone out from under his jaw, pushed the off button, then placed the receiver on the floor. How did he know the man in the picture? He slipped the photograph in his back pocket, then pushed the first of the three boxes against the wall. He could use the filler for holiday gifts, and the boxes might just come in handy, too. He piled the second box on top of the first. Then he bent down and grabbed the sides of the third box. He lifted it, and the bottom opened, spilling Styrofoam pieces onto the floor.

Great, now he would have to clean up that mess. Flipping the box around, he placed it on the floor and folded the flaps one over the other so they would stay closed. Then he bent down and started grabbing handfuls of the white kernels. That was when he saw the magazine. Kneeling down, Tony picked up the magazine. He checked out the issue date. It was two years old. Handsome, well built naked men with raging hardons stared up at him as he thumbed through the pages. A chill ran through him. It had to have been the last porn magazine the previous owner had bought before he'd been murdered. Tony closed the magazine, then placed it on the floor by his side. He didn't need to think about that. Plus, he had to get the Styrofoam back into the box, then stack it on top of the other boxes.

After Tony finished packing the Styrofoam back into the box, he looked down to see the magazine open to the personal ads. And there, under the Rhode Island header, was a single ad:

FULL SERVICE
Horny Rhode Island man in the Providence area looking to massage and service hung studs. Drop me a line if you're interested. Box 5624

Tony placed the photograph in the opened magazine, then closed it and went upstairs.

Tony woke from a crack of thunder. The curtains in the open window flew into the room like waving arms. Tony got up and bounded across the room, not giving a thought to his naked body being exposed to anyone who might be outside. Grabbing the window pane with his fingertips, he quickly pulled it down and shut out the wind and rain. The curtains slowly drifted back into place. Lightning struck, quickly flashing Tony's reflection in the window, and the reflection of another person behind him. There was a clap of thunder. Tony jumped, then quickly turned to look behind him. Nobody was there. It had to have been his imagination, or a trick of light casting his reflection twice. He slowly made his way back to bed, and slipped between the covers.

Rain beat against the window quickly, then died, then quickened again. Wind rushed around the outside of the house. It was a bad storm causing my imagination to work overtime, Tony thought. Nothing more than the storm.

Tony grabbed his nut sack, pulled it out from between his legs, then gave his shaft a playful stroke. He pulled the foreskin over his cock head, then closed his eyes and tried to tune out the whirlwind. Gently, he smoothed his fingertips over his stomach, and up the center of his pectorals the way Peter used to do it when they'd been together. The rubbing of his fingertips soothed him until he was in a half sleep. Then his hand rested on his stomach, and his breathing softened.

In his half sleep Tony felt something on his cock, like fingers rubbing the sensitive underside, moving along the length of his shaft, over the heart shaped head. It was a dream, Tony thought. The hand gripped his dick, then he felt warmth engulf the knob, then run down along his prick. Tony let out a groan, then separated his legs slightly. There was sucking, like he was getting blown. Hands caressed his inner thighs, the thumbs moving between his legs, below his balls. Then the hands slid in and fingers gripped his nut sack. There was a slight tug on his balls, and Tony let out a soft groan as he grabbed the edge of the mattress. The sucking continued, and the gentle tugging, driving Tony wild with lust. Hot spunk rose up in his cock, forming pressure at the ripe head.

Tony opened his eyes and stared into the darkness of the room. He wasn't dreaming. Someone was blowing him. His body tightened, and he tried not to blow his load. He didn't want to. Not yet. Looking down, he saw a head bobbing on his dick. Whoever it was was working his knob, sucking on it and smoothing his lips around the edge of the crown.

"Oh fuck," Tony said through clenched teeth. He gripped a handful of blanket and arched his back. He was lost in the sensation, and didn't want it to leave. But he couldn't hold back. The mouth slid down his prick, swallowing the entire length of his rod. Tony's breathing quickened. Lightning lit the room. Then there was a loud burst of thunder. Tony jumped, then felt the first squirt of cum spew from his piss slit. Tony grunted. He shot another load of hot spunk. "Fuck," Tony muttered as more of his ball juice burst free until he was spent.

Tony moved back on the bed. The man who had blown him wiped his long fingers over his lower lip and stretched his full lips into a grin. The man's blue plaid shirt fell open on either side of a smooth chest. Tony gasped as he made the connection between the man he'd seen on Benefit Street, the man in the photograph, and the man in his room. What did he want?

"Who are you?" Tony asked.

The man turned towards Tony, and his form became muted and slightly transparent. "My blood stains your floor," he said, then his form shifted into shadow and he disappeared.

Tony sat up, his heart thumping in his chest. It couldn't be. He looked down at his waning dick, then shot out of bed. He ran out of his bedroom and into the living room. *My blood stains your floor.* He threw on the overhead light. The stain was there, in the center of the floor. He went down on his knees and pressed his palm against the stain. This couldn't be happening.

Then he felt a hand gently smoothing his back. Tony sat up, his fingertips moving from the floorboards to his knee. The hands caressed his back, sliding around his chest. What now, Tony thought.

"Don't be afraid," a voice said. It was the same voice he'd heard at Waterfire. "I mean no harm."

Fingertips slowly drifted over Tony's chest, circling his nipples, soothing him.

I mean no harm.

Tony closed his eyes, then leaned back, feeling the man behind him support his weight, and allowed the hands to soothe him.

BACKSTAGE BLOW BUDDIES

I'd spent the early evening back stage wrapping Ed's thin, pale body in black silk. He'd already shaved himself down, so there wasn't a single hair on him other than his eyebrows and the dark peach fuzz on his head. His cock hung a thick six inches between his legs, and his big balls drooped in their skin pouch. Black socks covered his narrow feet.

I started at his left foot, wrapping the silk strip around his ankle, keeping the cloth tight and snug. The definition of Ed's calf became even more evident as the cloth was wound around it. It wasn't until I reached his crotch that I was able to stop, then grab the second strip of black satin.

I wrapped his right leg the same as his left, stopping once more when I reached Ed's meat, which hung at half mast. His knobby cock head bobbed only inches from my salivating mouth as I crisscrossed the two strips of cloth between his legs. All I could think of was taking that tube of flesh in my mouth and swallowing it whole.

Weaving the cloth between his legs, I held his cock down against his left thigh, covered the head with silk, then wound the strip across the downward curve of his ass. Then I held his balls against his right opposite thigh and wrapped them in the same manner.

Ed hummed an unrecognizable tune to himself as I wove the silk around his stomach, then higher, up over his pectorals. It wasn't until I reached his nickel sized nipples that I had to use the black aluminum clasps to secure the silk, then grab a new strip of black silk to begin to wrap his left arm.

Wrapping an arm is no different from wrapping a leg. It isn't a challenge until you get to the shoulder, but once you've figured out how to get the cloth to fit under the armpit and wrap back around the chest, you're in the clear. I worked on the right arm once the left was completed. The wrapping stopped at the neck, then was secured with another black clasp.

Once wrapped, Ed put on black leather biker boots that ran half way up his calf, a thick black leather dog collar, and matching leather wrist bands.

"How do I look?" he asked, hs voice deep and masculine.

Saying that he looked good wasn't enough to describe how the black silk accented the tight curve of his ass, and put the hefty package between his legs in prominent view without exposing a single inch of flesh. Even after having wrapped his body for the past twelve shows, I found him amazing to behold.

"You look great," Nick said, standing in the doorway and scanning Ed's magnificent body. Dropping his hands into the pockets of his beige chinos, Nick stepped into the dressing room. For a guy old enough to be Ed's father, Nick was handsome. Ed had once confessed that when he went out in public with Nick, people often mistook them for father and son. Since they both have well defined jaws and dark hair, Nick's tinged with gray, it wasn't shocking news.

"I've already started writing some new songs for our next CD," Ed said.

Nick walked up to the vacant ratan chair to the left of the vanity and took a seat. "Tell me about it."

Once Nick and Ed started talking, I figured it was time to get out of there and start dressing up for the show. When I got to the dressing room, Stan was sitting in a swivel chair in front of the mirror applying gel to his hair and combing it forward. It didn't look as if Stan was wearing any clothes. He wiped his hands off on a towel, then threw it on the shelf that ran the length of the mirror. The serpentine scar that went from his right ear to the center of his collar bone was reflected in the mirror as he turned to face me.

"Pretty boy all wrapped up?" Stan asked with a snarl.

"Sure is," I said, kicking off my sneakers. I still had to change up and wanted to make it quick.

Stan twirled the chair to face me, and I saw the black jock strap that covered his cock and balls. Stan sat back and watched as I pulled off my jeans and t-shirt. Once I was naked, he got up and stood inches away from me. He grabbed my balls and pulled them down quick, causing me to wince. The bottom of my shaft rubbed against Stan's arm.

"Did you get all hot for him while you were in there?" Stan asked, his voice low and hushed. His hot breath rushed against my face. "Did you want to suck his big old cock, just like everyone else who's coming to this shit box to see us play?" He gave my nuts another tug, and my knees bent slightly to ease the pain.

"Well?"

"Yes," I said.

Stan let go of my balls, then his hand flew up to grip my chin. He pushed me back against the wall, his forearm pressing against the center of my chest. Then he leaned up against me, and my stiff dick pressed against his thigh.

"You wanted to take his big old prick down your throat, but you didn't. Isn't that right?"

"Yes," I said.

Letting go of my chin, Stan stepped back. The tip of his thin dick stuck out the left side of his jock strap, a pearl of precum glistening off the piss slit. Stan gave the side of my face a firm, yet gentle slap, then slipped his hand around the back of my neck. Lunging forward, he pressed his lips against mine and pushed his tongue into my mouth. He moved back, wiped spit off his lips, then grabbed his crotch. "Get down on your knees and suck my cock," Stan said.

I did as I was told. Stan pulled his meat out of his jock strap and slapped it against my face. "You fucking pig," he said. "Take it in your mouth." Grabbing my head, he stuffed his shaft down my gullet, then started pumping it in and out of my face.

Then, when Stan was about to blow his load, he pulled his wet dick out of my mouth and stroked it over my face. "You little cock sucker," he hissed, then blasted his first shot on my nose. "Fuck, man." Another glob splashed against my left cheek. His body jolted, then the rest of his hot spunk shot onto my cheeks and chin.

Stan gave me a shove, and I fell onto my back against the cold tile floor. "I want to see you jerk off," Stan said, spreading out next to me. I jerked my hard cock as Stan licked his spunk off my face. "You like that, don't you, you little fuck," Stan said, the scent of cum on his breath. "You like to have guys squirt their loads on your face."

"Yes," I said, feeling my shaft fill with hot jizm.

"Too bad Ed won't give it to you. Little prissy Ed."

Stan was right; I did wish Ed would squirt his load on my face some day. The mere thought made me stroke my shaft even faster.

"You're a fucking pig."

"Yes, I am."

"You want to suck Ed's cock."

"Yes."

"Feel his balls against your chin."

"I do." My cock was ready to blow. I felt it in my legs, and the head of my dick. Stan twisted my left nipple between his thumb and index finger. "Come on, you little shit," he hissed. "Blow your load for Eddie." That was when I shot my load, covering my stomach and chest.

Stan stood as I tried to catch my breath. "It's time to get dressed," he said.

Stan and I were dressed in leather pants and sleeveless black cotton shirts. Standing in the foreground, in front of the wild, screaming crowd, was Ed. The black silk bandages encasing Ed's body were moist with sweat and gleamed in the light as he clutched the microphone in front of his mouth and sung the final lines before my guitar riff. Stan lightened his beat on the drums, then looked my way and grimaced. Ed turned to the side, his bulging cock and balls glistening, and bowed his head.

My fingers danced along the guitar frets, striking each chord as the metal tip of my thumb screamed out the song in all its agony. Leaning back, I let my body dance with the music. I gave the strings a final strum, then lifted my hand and let the guitar music fade out. The crowd went wild, whistling and clapping.

When the clapping wound down, Ed stepped back up and took the spotlight. Stan spat to the side, twirled a drumstick in his right hand, then went back to a soft, steady beat on the drums. I played the same low, haunting melody on the guitar. Ed began to sing, his voice low and cynical:

You've gone down, where you want to be
you've gone down, and that's fine with me
you've gone down, you've gone down on me.

Stan changed into jeans and a t-shirt, then was out the door before I had my pants off. I assumed he'd gone out to find the hottest club or bar in town, since that was what he liked doing after a show. Me, well, after each show I tended to unwrap Ed, then go back to my room and jerk off thinking about what I wished would happen. After each performance, it became clear that Ed didn't want me sexually. The silly thing was, that I still hadn't given up hope.

I'd seen Ed talking to Nick back stage after the show, so I had time to get changed up before heading to his dressing room to help him unwrap. I threw on a pair of pants and a plaid shirt that I didn't bother to button because I was still hot from the stage lights, then went to Ed's dressing room. When I arrived in the dressing room, Ed was standing in front of Nick, who sat on the ratan chair, his hand rubbing Ed's firm ass. Nick looked at me as I closed the door.

"Come on in," Nick said, not moving his hand from Ed's ass. "You boys put on a good show tonight."

Ed turned towards me, his swollen cock head peeking out from between the strips of silk. "I loved your solo," he said.

I blushed, feeling proud and embarrassed for having walked in on Nick and Ed about to fuck. Feeling the need to retreat, I grabbed the doorknob.

"You don't have to go," Nick said.

Ed stepped up to me, placed his hand gently on my left hip and whispered in my ear, "Nick would like to see us together."

My cock sprung to attention. Reaching out, I pressed my palm against his waist and felt the warm silk. Ed licked my lips, and I slipped my hand around to the small of his back, then lower, feeling the outward curve of his ass. We kissed again, and I sucked on his tongue.

"Come here," Ed said, taking a few steps back. He parted the silk that covered his crotch, then pulled out his thick dick and heavy balls. His shaft rose up stiff in front of black silk.

I can't tell you how badly I wanted to touch Ed's prick, or swallow every inch of his dick. I snuck a peek at Nick, who had his long, uncut shaft in his grip.

"Why don't you take off your clothes?" Nick said.

I glanced at Ed as he stroked his hardening prick, then shook his head at me. "I know you want it," Ed said. "You've been drooling over my cock since we started this tour."

There were hands slipping around my waist, drifting under my t-shirt, pulling it up and over my head. Nick had gotten up from the chair and was behind me, undressing me. He started unbuttoning my jeans. I kicked off my sneakers. My jeans fell to the floor, and Nick started rubbing my chest, then pinching my nipples.

"Pinch them harder," I said.

Nick gave my nipples a hard twist, making me pull in air from the sudden jolt of pain. Then Ed grabbed my nuts and cock and pulled them towards him, then gave me a hard kiss. Nick stopped pinching my tits, and placed his hand on my ass, smoothing his fingers into the crack. I spread my legs and he dipped his middle finger deeper in the crack, feeling my tight little fuck hole.

"I want to see you suck his cock," Nick said. "You want that?"

"Yes," I said.

Nick pushed his middle finger up my ass, then pulled it out and placed it under my nose. The sweet smell of ass filled my nostrils. Then Nick stuffed his middle finger into my mouth, forcing it down my throat, then plunged it back up my ass. I spread my legs further as he finger fucked my ass nice and slow. "You like that," Nick said.

"Yes," I said.

"You like getting it up the ass." Nick shoved two more fingers into my hole, spreading it open.

"He has a nice mouth, too," Ed said, shoving three fingers down my gullet. He slid his fingers out of my mouth and wiped them dry on my face.

I practically panted with lust, I was so eager to get down on my knees and start sucking on Ed's big prod. Nick pulled his finger out of my ass, then I went down on my knees and grabbed Ed's thick shaft. The bulbous head stuck out from inside my fist, and I gave it a lick before stuffing it into my mouth. Ed's prick was so thick, and the head alone filled my mouth to capacity. I wondered if I would be able to take the entire length down my throat.

Nick stood to the left and stroked his prick as Ed placed his hand on my head and guided his cock down my throat nice and slow. Ed pulled out until the head was rubbing against my lips. Then he plunged it back down my throat, causing me to gag and sputter before pulling it out. He rammed it back down my gullet, and I gulped and swallowed every last inch of his meat. Spit surrounded my lips as he fucked my mouth until it ached.

I pulled back, and Ed's cock spilled out of my mouth. Ed rubbed his meat against my face. "You need a rest?" Ed asked.

"Just some air," I said. "I'm okay."

Ed poked his swollen cock head against my lips. I opened my mouth, and he plunged his shaft down my gullet and held it there. Ed's balls were against my chin as I kept my throat relaxed. Ed pulled his hips back only slightly and jabbed at my throat. His cock head swelled even more, and I thought he was going to blow his load directly into my stomach.

Then Ed pulled out. I gulped air. Thick drool dripped from Ed's dick as he grabbed it and gave it a few strokes. Then I started gulping Nick's shaft. Nick grabbed a lock of my hair and started fucking my throat good and hard.

"I'm going to cum," Ed said.

I stopped sucking Nick's dick to watch Ed's fist quickly pistoning his prick. Keeping my face close to Ed's purple knob, I hoped he would shoot his creamy load on my face. Ed's breathing became quick, then he let out a groan. Hot globs of spunk hit the side of my face, then my neck. By the time Ed was finished, I had his ball juice dripping off my jaw and down my shoulder. There were slow drips of spunk running down my chest, reaching my nipple.

Ed grabbed a towel off the vanity and wiped his hand before tossing it to me. I wiped the cum off my face.

Standing up, I felt Nick's arms around my waist, pulling my back against him. "I want to fuck you," he said, rubbing his shaft in the crack of my ass.

Unwrapping Nick's arms from my body, I walked over to the vanity and leaned against it. In the mirror, I watched Nick and Ed approach. Ed separated my ass cheeks and fingered my pucker as Nick searched through his pants. He pulled out a condom, and put it on. Ed stuffed three fingers up my hole, slowly gliding them in and out, getting it ready for Nick's prod to give it a good work out.

Pulling his fingers out of my ass, Ed stepped to the side. Nick positioned himself behind me. He slapped his cock against my hole, then plunged it deep within my bowels with one quick gut wrenching thrust. My eyes watered and I nearly gasped. Nick fucked me good and hard, his hips slapping against my ass. In the mirror I saw Ed's satin clad body as he watched Nick work my butt.

"Shit, you have a hot ass," Nick said, his voice low.

Ed crouched down beneath me and started licking the length of my dick. Then he gripped the shaft and sucked on the head. Man, I was in my glory getting it up the ass and having Ed suck my prick. It wasn't long before I felt myself ready to blow. Clenching my teeth, I tried to hold my orgasm in check. Ed must have figured out that I was close because he took his mouth off my cock head and started stroking my rod with quick glides that matched Nick's fucking.

Then I felt Nick's cock twitch, and he let out a groan. His thrusts started slowing. "Fuck," he hissed, then his cock head pulsed up my fuck chute, and I knew he was spewing his creamy spunk up my ass.

That was when I blew my load. Closing my eyes, I shot in pulsing blasts as Nick finished spewing the last of his spunk. When I had finished coming, I looked down to see thin white stripes of jizm against black silk. I had shot all over Ed's body, and the result was like a well defined black and white painting.

Nick pulled his shaft out of my ass and discarded the cum filled condom as Ed stood in front of me. "I won't be wearing this again," Ed said, not that he'd ever worn the same strips of silk twice.

"Where's Stan tonight?" Nick asked.

"He's out. Probably at some club or bar trying to get laid," I said.

"Why don't you bring him here after the show some time?" Ed said. "I bet we can teach that bad boy a thing or two."

I smiled and nodded. The mere mention of the four of us together was enough to get my dick hard again.

GUY TROUBLE

Guy's open shirt flapped like gentle wings as a soft breeze cooled his chest, making his nipples hard. Rubbing his toes against the bottom of his sandals, he felt the small blunted points massage the tips, then hoisted his backpack over his shoulder. Just a freshman in college, and already Guy knew he was going to get himself into trouble. If only he wasn't sharing a room with the most handsome guy on campus, Wallace Stevens. It wouldn't be so bad if Wallace wasn't so damn straight, always out running or playing ball with his friends, and shamelessly undressing in front of him. It was just so damn difficult for Guy not to turn his head to watch Wallace every time he pulled off his shirt and exposed his hairy, muscular chest. A thin line of hair led to the elasticized waist of his boxer shorts. If he had to room with a straight guy, why couldn't it be with some nerdy type?

Guy scratched his firm stomach, then stepped through the arched opening that looked as if it had once been used for horse drawn carriages to pass through, and walked towards the college green. Brick colonial buildings surrounded the green, which was crisscrossed by narrow paved paths that led between buildings and to openings in the wrought iron fence. People lounged out on the grass, and a shirtless threesome of men played frisbee next to a modern sculpture of what appeared to be some type of globular stone chair. Two of the frisbee playing boys were bronzed by the sun. The third, a tall African American man with nickel sized nipples and a firm stomach eyed the two other boys suspiciously before throwing the frisbee into the air and watching it coast above the head of the boy on the left with the torn denim shorts and no shoes. The shoeless boy jumped into the air, right arm outstretched to grasp the edge of the white disc. Then the boy fell back to the ground, his bare feet planted firmly on the grass with his knees bent slightly.

What a beautiful sight those boys were, but they wouldn't be outside for much longer. Soon the nights would begin to cool down, and the mornings would become too nippy for shorts and t-shirts. Guy walked past a few boys lounging out, talking with friends and reading. Guy's thick cock began to stir, and he quickened his pace. The last thing he wanted to do was pop a boner, especially since he hadn't had any clean underwear, so he'd just slipped into his khaki walking shorts before heading out.

Once through the gate, Guy took a left and walked past the stone church, then further to the long three-story brick building where his dorm room was located. Guy's roommate had invited him to play a game of basketball with him and his friends earlier that morning, but he'd declined the offer. He'd already had too much to get done before classes really started.

Walking through the dimly lit halls to his room, Guy kept his fingers crossed, hoping that Wallace wasn't around. He really needed to blow his load. The door to their room was in front of him. Reaching out, he turned the knob and the door opened. Guy threw the door open, to find Wallace standing in front of their unmade bunk beds in a faded pair of paisley boxer shorts. Scratching his damp hair, Wallace let out a huff. "Close the door, please."

Guy closed the door.

Sweat glistened off the hair on Wallace's chest, driving Guy wild with lust. Hoping to hide his arousal, Guy dropped his books in front of the cheap desk and took a seat. He tried not to watch as Wallace slid off his boxer shorts and walked over to the closet to grab a threadbare towel. Guy peeked at Wallace's firm ass, and the soft hair that lined the crack. If only he could get down on his knees and bury his face between those beautiful mounds of flesh.

"You should have come. We could have used another player." Wallace wrapped the towel around his waist, the length of his shaft slightly evident beneath the cloth.

"Did you win?"

"No. We let the other team have the extra guy," Wallace said. "We would have won if you were on our side, though."

"Don't be so sure, I'm a little rusty," Guy said.

"I bet you're still better than those other guys." Wallace padded over to the door and opened it. "I'll be in the shower."

The door closed. Guy was alone in the room. Wallace's boxer shorts were on the floor. Guy reached out and touched the soft cotton material, which was slightly damp in the crotch. Flipping the boxer shorts inside out, Guy brought the crotch to his nose and inhaled. They smelled of Wallace's crotch. Moving the seam of the boxer shorts further, he inhaled where Wallace's asshole had rested. How sweet it smelled. Guy wanted to lick the boxer shorts, but didn't. He didn't want to leave any tell tale signs of his actions.

Leaning back, Guy rested the shorts on his face, reached between his legs and felt his stiff dick. If only he could be smelling the real thing. What a joy it would be to have Wallace resting his sweaty balls over his face, have them hanging in his mouth. Guy knew he would be able to fit both balls in his mouth, close his lips around them and suck.

Guy pulled his cock out from the bottom of his shorts, rubbing the underside of the swollen head with his thumb. If Wallace did let him suck his nuts, he would be so happy that he'd even lick behind them, run the tip of his tongue along that thin fleshy cord leading to his puckered fuck hole. He could rub his fingers inside the moist, furry crack. How great it would be to have Wallace blow his load all over his chest and neck.

Guy's body tightened. Hot spurts of cum shot out of his swollen knob, splashed against his knee, then slowly dripped down his leg.

Standing outside of the Avon Cinema, Guy looked up at the triangular marquee with the evening's movies and show times.

"Hey." It was Wallace's deep voice coming from behind him. Guy turned. "Want to shoot some hoops, one on one?"

"I don't know." He'd have to change into sneakers, he did not want to play wearing boat shoes.

"It beats sitting alone watching a movie," Wallace said.

Guy shrugged. "I'm not wearing sneakers."

"Go and change. Come on, it will be fun," Wallace said. "Roommate bonding time. I can meet you there."

Guy agreed, then started walking to the dorm. It wasn't going to do any harm to shoot a few hoops with Wallace. Although it had been a while since he'd played basketball, the game was sure to come back to him, like anything else. And he'd be able to get a good look at Wallace's naked body again once they got back to the dorm and showered. He could sneak a few looks at Wallace without being noticed; he'd done it before. If he was good about it, he wouldn't get himself into trouble. Guy quickened his pace. It took him no time to get back to the dorm, change into sneakers and head out to the basketball courts to find Wallace slowly dribbling the ball.

"That was pretty quick," Wallace said. He threw the ball at Guy, who caught it.

"I'm a little rusty," Guy said as he began to dribble the ball. "Don't laugh if I fuck up."

"We'll just shoot, no heavy competition."

Dribbling the ball, Guy positioned himself for an easy hoop shot. He stood a few feet in front of the hoop, bounced the ball. Eyed the hoop. Bounced the ball, then caught it. The ball was light in his grasp as he held it, reached up on his toes and tossed it. The ball arched, then dropped into the hoop, making a swooshing sound as it slipped through the net.

Wallace ran for the ball, bounced it between his legs, then dribbled it over towards Guy. "Block me. Come on." Wallace moved around Guy, the ball making a hollow sound every time it hit pavement.

This was it, Guy had to play. Guy chased Wallace around the court, arms extended to block any possible hoop shots. But Wallace was too quick, and soon jumped, tossed the ball and got it through the hoop. Both men ran after the ball, but this time Guy had it. He ran dribbling the ball with Wallace staying close by his side. Guy turned, stopped, then moved again. But Wallace was on him, blocking his every chance to shoot.

"You want it, don't you?" Wallace said.

Guy couldn't believe what he was hearing. But it was about getting the ball through the hoop, and not anything more than that. He rushed down the court, towards the opposite hoop. Wallace was on top of him, his hot breath rushing past Guy's face. "Does it matter where it goes?" Guy asked.

"Just get it in," Wallace said.

Guy tossed the ball, getting a perfect net shot.

"Awesome!" Wallace said, grabbing hold of Guy's left shoulder and giving it a firm squeeze. "That was one impressive maneuver."

Wallace went for the ball this time, and the two men kept playing. Each time Wallace blocked Guy, he asked how bad Guy wanted to make it, or if Guy thought he'd be able to get it in. It drove Guy wild, and kept him aroused and energized throughout their play.

By the time Wallace and Guy stopped playing, they were both

hot and out of breath. Beads of sweat covered Wallace's upper lip and brow. Wallace wrapped his right arm around Guy's shoulders, pulling him in close. "That was fun."

Guy fought the urge to return the hug in kind. He had to stay calm, and never get aroused. "Sure was."

Wallace unwrapped his arm from Guy's shoulders, then the two men started to walk back to their dorm room. Knowing Wallace was hot and sweaty next to him, and that soon the both of them would be in their room getting ready to shower made Guy's cock stir. Guy paid close attention to the street to keep his mind away from Wallace's sweaty body. They walked down Hope Street, past apartment houses, then turned right onto Angel Street, past a restaurant on their left, then turned at the corner of Angel and Thayer streets.

"You're quiet," Wallace said.

"I'm just tired," Guy said. They were only a block away from the dorms.

"Not used to playing around like that, huh?" Wallace gave Guy a friendly punch on the shoulder. "You'll feel better once we get to the dorm."

"I'm not going to crash or anything," Guy said. "Just have to sit for a little bit."

"Sure."

Guy pushed his hands inside his pockets to hide his stiffening dick.

The brick dorm building was in sight. When they reached the door, Wallace fished out his key and held the door open for Guy. They walked to their room, then Guy opened the door. Guy took a seat on the bottom bunk bed and watched as Wallace kicked off his sneakers without untying them. Then Wallace grabbed the bottom of his t-shirt and pulled it up over his head, exposing his hairy chest and the damp hair under his arms.

"You taking a shower, or are you planning on standing around stinking all day?" Wallace said, tossing his shirt on the floor.

"Give me a second," Guy said, lying back on the bed with his feet still planted on the floor. He couldn't bare to watch Wallace step out of his shorts, or even the brief outline of his cock and balls in his boxer shorts.

"Hey," Wallace said.

Guy felt damp cotton on his face, then the scent of Wallace's sweaty balls. He grabbed the boxer shorts and threw them back at Wallace before sitting up to see Wallace standing in front of him with his big shaft at half mast.

"Your second is up," Wallace said. "Time to shower."

Guy untied his sneakers, then kicked them under the bed. When he stood, he hoped his shaft didn't look too aroused. Wallace stood back, leaning against the edge of the desk as Guy pulled off his t-shirt. He tried not to look at Wallace, or even think of how sexy it made him feel to take his clothes off in front of another man. He reached for his shorts, unzipped them, and let them fall to the floor.

"How come you never played with us before?" Wallace asked, looking to the left, at the window that looked out onto the street.

"Never had time," Guy said, knowing that if he took off his BVDs he would get an erection.

"You need to make some time." Wallace brushed past him, then stepped up the ladder to the top bunk bed. "I'm going to use the same towel I used this morning."

Every muscle in Wallace's hairy legs stretched as he stood on the ladder and reached for what Guy assumed to be his towel. Wallace's firm ass looked delicious, too. Guy's cock was now fully hard; he had to stop staring. He pulled off his socks, then looked up. Wallace was making his way down the ladder. His shaft was at half mast and Wallace was almost standing beside him. Guy pulled the chair away from the desk and took a seat. His hardon had to go away before Wallace was able to notice.

"Showering in your underwear?" Wallace said, wrapping the deep green towel around his waist.

Guy stood, pretending not to notice his erection, then pulled off his white BVDs. He had a towel in the closet near the door. Guy opened the closet, stood on tip toe and pulled a blue and white striped towel down. Wallace's hand was on his back, and his other hand reached out on the shelf. Guy felt the thick towel around Wallace's waist rub against him, then drift down to the floor. Then Wallace's hand was lower on his back, just above his ass as he pulled a fresh towel off the shelf.

"I should probably use a clean towel," Wallace said.

Guy felt Wallace's stiff dick brush up against his own. He looked down, then felt Wallace's hand rubbing the curve of his ass. Guy dropped the towel.

"You going to pick that up?" Wallace asked.

Slowly, Guy went down on his knees. Wallace's thick shaft was in front of him, a bead of precum on the piss slit. Guy leaned in close and inhaled the scent of sweaty balls, then stuck his tongue between the ball sack and Wallace's upper thigh.

"Yes, suck my balls," Wallace whispered. "Suck my sweaty balls."

Guy sucked Wallace's balls into his mouth and closed his lips around them as he reached between Wallace's legs and rubbed his middle finger against his tight fuck hole.

Wallace stroked his shaft a few times. "Oh man, play with that hole. Oh, that feels real good."

Guy pulled the nuts out of his mouth, then sniffed his middle finger. Wallace's hole smelled so sweet and tasty. Wallace grabbed Guy's wrist and pulled him onto his feet. Wallace sucked Guy's middle finger, leaving it moist with spit when it came out of his mouth.

Guy put his finger between Wallace's legs, found the tight hole and pressed against it. Wallace spread his legs further apart, and Guy's finger moved inside. Wallace tightened his hole, grabbing Guy's finger with his sphincter and holding it tight. Soon Guy felt Wallace's thick cock slapping him in the face. He opened his mouth and started sucking his cock, feeling it plunge down his gullet, then fuck his throat with long, slow strokes.

Guy pulled the cock out of his mouth, then rubbed it over his face as he inserted a second finger up Wallace's fuck hole. Wallace sighed and moaned. Guy couldn't believe how much Wallace liked being finger fucked, and thought he'd really like to have his cock shoved up his ass.

Guy stood, grabbed Wallace's nuts and gently pulled down on them. Wallace winced, then leaned in and kissed him on the lips. Guy reached around and gently spanked Wallace's firm ass. Then he grabbed Wallace's ass with both hands, one on each cheek, and separated the two fleshy mounds. "I want to fuck you," Guy said.

Wallace sighed. "I have a condom in my sock drawer."

"Go get it."

Wallace stepped over to the bureau near the bunk beds and

grabbed a condom and a tube of lubricant.

"Put it on my cock," Guy said, and soon Wallace was on his knees unrolling the latex sheath over his rod, then lubing it up.

"Grab the top bunk and spread your legs," Guy said, and Wallace did just that.

Guy slapped Wallace's ass a few times, then grabbed the lubricant and slathered some on his pucker. He couldn't wait to feel his prod push inside that tight fuck hole. He spanked Wallace's hole with his shaft. "Tell me you want it," Guy said.

"I want you to fuck me," Wallace said.

"Beg."

"Please."

Guy positioned his cock head against the tight hole, but didn't push inside, instead he rubbed the head around.

"Please."

"Please what?" Guy asked.

"Fuck me, please. Shove your cock up my ass."

With one swift shove, Guy planted his shaft all the way inside Wallace's warm bowels. Wallace let out a groan, then Guy pulled back and started to fuck him with long, hard jabs. Guy had to grab hold of Wallace's hips to keep himself steady. And Wallace moaned and continued to ask for it. "Fuck me hard, man. Oh yeah, give me that big old dick."

Soon Guy was close to letting his load shoot. He reached around and felt Wallace's stiff dick. "Man, don't touch it," Wallace said. "I'll fucking cum right here and now." That was all Guy had to hear. He wrapped his fingers around Wallace's shaft and felt it twitch. "Fuck!" Wallace cried as he blew his load.

And that was when Guy felt his cock head pulse as he shot his spunk.

When they were finished coming, Guy pulled his cock out of Wallace's ass, then peeled off the rubber. He tossed the condom into the trash can to the left of the desk. Then Guy felt Wallace's hand around the back of his neck, pulling him in close for a kiss. "You're one hot fuck," Wallace said once their lips parted.

"Maybe we should play ball more often," Guy said.

Wallace grinned. "That we should, man. That we should."

FARM BOY FUCKFEST

L ance woke up while the rooster crowed. Kicking off the sheets, he grabbed his stiff seven inch dick at the base, feeling the thick bush of wiry brown pubic hair against his big hand, and gave it a slow upward stroke. When he reached the ripe cock head, he rubbed his palm around it, then stroked back down. Holding his shaft at the base, he thumped it against his stomach a few times.

Lance's big balls hung low between his legs, and he gave them a tug with his free hand. Wrapping his thumb and index finger tight around the hairy sack, he pulled down until his balls felt as if they were going to be yanked off his body. He spread his legs further and let out a hoarse groan.

Precum drooled out of his piss slit and filled his navel. He took his hand off his shaft and plunged his middle finger into his belly button, scooping out the thick juicy fluid and brought it to his lips. It tasted so damn good. Moving his nuts to the side, he spread his ass cheeks and poked at his sweaty butt hole. He pushed his middle finger inside, then inserted a second.

He wished it was his cousin Al's friend, Dan, poking at his fuck hole. Dan was so tall, and his chest had a thick coat of dark hair that ran over his well formed pecs and firm stomach. His nickel size nipples were always hard. Dan always wore tight button fly jeans that looked about to burst open at the crotch. The first time Lance had seen Dan with Al at the local bar, he thought he was a new hand at the ranch. But he wasn't. Dan was some hot shot city lawyer from Los Angeles who had decided to move to a small New England town for a pleasant change of pace.

Lance imagined feeling Dan's scruffy beard rub between his thighs as he sucked his nuts into his mouth, wrapping his lips around the sack and pulling back. How good it would feel to have Dan's thick fingers pressed into his thigh, spreading his legs open wide to expose his pucker. He wondered how good it would feel to have a guy's cock buried up his ass.

Lance grabbed his dick, then slowly stroked it as he fucked his ass with both index and middle fingers. More precum spilled out the slit at the tip of his cock head, which was ripe and ready to burst. All it took was the final upward stroke to cause his legs to tighten, his back to arch, and the first spray of hot cum to shoot out of his piss slit. Lance let out a guttural groan as he emptied his ball juice all over his chest and stomach.

Still thinking about Dan, Lance rubbed the cooling cum into his skin. A man like Dan would never do what Lance wanted. As it was, Lance had never found anyone who might even come close, not that he'd ever really sought out anyone who might. Perhaps if he'd lived in some big city it would be easier. He'd heard about guys in cities who would do just about anything. He'd fantasized about going to New York or Los Angeles before, but didn't want to go alone. And if he went with a friend, it might be found out that he wanted to suck dick.

Reaching towards the floor, Lance picked up the underwear he'd worn the day before and gave them a sniff. They smelled of stale ball sweat and musty ass. The scent brought his dick back to life, but he didn't have time to give his cock another whirl.

Someone started knocking on the bedroom window. Lance slipped the underwear on, then padded across the room. He pulled the dusty blind open. Just across the field, the sun was rising. And there was Al, in his typical red plaid shirt and worn out jeans. His blond hair was uncombed, and it didn't seem as if he'd bothered to shower.

"Looks like you need someone to help you take care of business, Lance," Al said, pointing at the areas of dried cum that frosted Lance's stomach.

"I've never seen girls hanging around you, so don't go pointing fingers," Lance said. "You got that feed for my cows?"

"In the truck," Al said.

"Why don't you come in and make some coffee while I wash up," Lance said, then stepped away from the window.

Light from the bathroom window hit the plastic shower curtain that surrounded the claw-foot tub and cast a blue tinge on Lance's skin. With his back to the hot spray, Lance wet his hair, then began to lather his smooth chest, then lower. His shaft sprung to life when he started to clean off his nuts. He imagined Dan in the shower with him, grabbing his balls from behind. How good Dan's cock would feel rubbing between his ass cheeks, getting ready to spray hot spunk on his back. Lance would lean back, feel the hair on Dan's chest against his back. Feel Dan's hot breath against his neck.

Lance didn't have time to jerk off, never mind clean up yet another sticky mess. Al was in his kitchen waiting for him so they could get that feed to the barn. Lance lathered his arm pits quick, rinsed, then turned off the shower.

The last of the feed had been loaded into the far corner of the barn. The barn smelled of hay and feed. The steady pump of the machinery sounded as the cows were milked. One cow let out a long moo, then another followed. Al and Lance walked outside. The air was slightly brisk, and the rows of corn a few feet away rustled as a breeze rushed past. To the left of the cornfield was the pumpkin patch, which stretched out behind the barn. It was such a beautiful sight, and Lance couldn't imagine leaving it to go live in some big city, no matter how easy it would be to get a man in bed.

"Dan was asking about your farm," Al said.

"If he ever wants to drop in and help pick corn, he's more than welcome," Lance said.

"I think he just wants to drop in on you, say hello and take a look around." Al stuffed his hands in his pockets, then took a step forward. "He said he was curious about how a guy can live off a farm, and he wants to see the pumpkins. He's never seen them on the vine before."

"He can come stare at them for as long as he likes." Imagining Dan staring at pumpkins made Lance grin. Then he imagined Dan naked, on his knees in front of him in the pumpkin patch. "There really isn't much to look at," Dan said to get his mind off the image of Dan naked. His dick was already stiff in his jeans.

"He's just curious," Al said.

"Is he?"

Al turned towards Lance and grinned. "Sure is. He's curious about a lot of things."

Lance knew his hardon was obvious, but there wasn't much he could do about it. After Al had left, he'd jerked off. Dan and Al were dropping by early to see the farm before sunset. The mere thought of Dan coming over made Lance's dick come back to life.

Standing in front of the porcelain kitchen sink, Lance washed the last of the supper dishes. His house was so old, there was no way Dan would be impressed by it. The walls in the eat-in kitchen needed a fresh coat of paint, and the small table was dull, and unsteady. The yellowed wallpaper in the living room was rolling up in a few corners, and the ranch style furniture looked dusty even after he vacuumed the thick brown cloth weave. And all the woodwork was dark brown, which always made the room look dark. Even the wood that encased the hulking mass of a television sitting against the far wall to the left of the sofa was dark. And the television was so old that it had two dials for choosing a channel. Lance didn't even know if it worked. He couldn't think of the last time he'd sat down to watch it.

Dropping onto the sofa, he stared out the picture window. Outside was a nice view of his front yard, the road and trees across from his house. The leaves on the trees were beginning to turn shades of red, and would be falling soon. Once they fell he'd have to rake them into piles that smelled of the richness of nature.

There was no use mulling over the outside. Lance stood, wiped his hands on his firm ass, then stepped into the kitchen. Even if Dan wasn't going to be impressed with his house, he could at least make sure it was clean. Lance's shaft rubbed against the inside of his jeans, and he grabbed it and squeezed. He wondered how long Dan would be able to hack living in the country, especially after spending so much time in that fast-paced city.

By the time Al and Dan arrived, Lance had cleaned the house from top to bottom. Lance's cock was rock hard, running down his leg and bulging out from inside his jeans. Although he tried, he couldn't keep his eyes off Dan's body. Dan wore a tight knit shirt that clung to his chest, exposing his hard nipples through the soft cloth. His jeans were tight, as usual, and his cock and balls pushed out, causing the button fly to bulge out.

"This is your place!" Dan said, extending his hand for a shake. Lance and Dan shook hands, then Dan stepped inside, followed by Al.

"It isn't much," Lance said, feeling the first drops of precum moisten his boxer shorts. "This is the dining room." Lance walked through the house, showing each room to them, hoping Dan didn't think he was just some hick.

"It looks comfortable," Dan said. "What I really want to see is the farm itself, though."

Al slid his hand under his gray sweatshirt and scratched his stomach. "He's been talking about wanting to see your pumpkins for the past week."

Dan grinned at Al, then gave Lance a wink. "I'm intrigued by farms."

"Well then, let's head out before it gets too dark to see anything," Lance said.

The sun was about to set by the time they were out in the pumpkin patch. Walking between the rows, Dan kept looking down as if amazed by the orange globes attached to green stems that spotted the ground.

Al squeezed Dan's shoulder and laughed. "Looks like the city boy's amazed!"

Dan went down on his knees, looking at the pumpkin at his feet. He placed his open hand on the smooth orange surface, then looked up at Lance, who stood only inches away from him. Lance fought the image of his shaft poking between Dan's lips. It was bad enough that he was standing in front of him with a raging boner in his pants.

"It's beautiful," Dan said.

Lance's shaft twitched. "You can have it, if you want," Lance said. The tip of Lance's cock head leaked more precum, and a small dab of the fluid spotted his jeans. Between Dan's beard and mustache, his lips looked inviting. Lance had to stop thinking about having sex with Dan, so he glanced at his cousin. Al was also packing a chubby.

"It's pretty impressive, isn't it?" Al said to Dan.

"Everything about this place is impressive," Dan said, glancing up at Lance as if eyeing his crotch. Lance assumed it was all in his head, Dan couldn't have just sized him up like that. Then Dan reached up, his hand dangling just over Lance's stiff dick. "Help me up, there," Dan said.

Lance took Dan's hand, and helped him to his feet. Reaching around, Dan gave Lance's ass a firm pat. Lance met Dan's gaze, and was unable to control himself any longer. Leaning forward, he gently placed his lips against Dan's. Dan slid his tongue between Lance's lips, then slid it out. Then he felt Dan's firm grip on his shaft, rubbing it through the cloth of his jeans. Lance thought he would blow his load right then and there, so he stepped back.

Al stood behind Dan, and pulled at his shirt, lifting it up over Dan's head. Both Dan and Al kissed long and hard. Watching the two men kiss, Lance felt as if he was participating in a sexual fantasy. Al's hands unbuttoned Dan's jeans, pulling them down to expose Dan's thick cock, which rose up seven inches from the base. Dan's balls were big and hairy, hanging low between his legs. Al grabbed Dan's meat and shook it. "You want to suck it?" he asked.

Without a word, Lance went down on his knees and took Dan's cock between his lips. The head alone filled his mouth, and he didn't think he'd be able to fit the entire length down his gullet. But Dan held the back of his head and eased the entire length of his meat down his throat. Just as smoothly as the shaft went in, it slid out, then back in.

Lance's cock was aching, begging to be let out as he eagerly sucked Dan's shaft. Then Al was beside Lance, and Dan pulled his prick out of his mouth. A thin strand of spit formed a line from the tip of Dan's cock to Lance's lips, then broke. Turning towards Al, Dan slapped his wet cock against Al's lips, then plunged his rod down his throat. Al looked real nice gulping down that thick slab of meat as Dan's nuts slapped against his chin.

Standing next to Dan, Lance gave him a kiss. Dan dipped his hand inside Lance's jeans, moving his middle finger up and down the crack of his ass. Lance stood on tip toe so Dan could get his hand further into his jeans.

"Pull your pants down, man," Dan said.

Lance undid his jeans and let them fall to his ankles. Dan's fingers dipped between Lance's ass cheeks and sought out his sweaty fuck hole. It felt so good having Dan probe his tight pucker with his fingers. Lance reached back and separated his ass cheeks, then Dan pressed two fingers against the hole and pushed them inside. Lance let out a sigh, feeling the first knuckle move inside his ass, then the second. Slowly Dan finger fucked Lance's fuck hole. He inserted three fingers deep inside Lance's pucker, which drove him wild with lust.

"Your ass feels so good," Dan whispered. "Let me fuck you."

"Yes," Lance said, looking down to see Al take Dan's shaft out of his mouth.

Reaching down, Dan struggled to grab a condom from the pocket of his jeans. He unrolled it over his shaft as Lance leaned forward and placed his hands on his knees. Then Lance felt Dan's tongue lapping at his pucker. Dan spit on the hole, licked at it some more, then stood up and slapped his sheathed prod against the hole.

"Take a deep breath," Al said.

Lance inhaled, then held his breath. Dan's shaft opened his asshole, stretching it tight around the thick rod. Slowly, Lance exhaled. Then there was a jabbing pain in his guts, and he let out a groan.

"It's okay there, pal," Dan said, reaching around and rubbing Lance's stomach. He eased more of his cock up Lance's fuck hole, then paused when his entire prick was buried deep inside.

Lance heard a wrapper being opened, then saw Al unrolling a condom over his cock. Al walked behind Dan.

"Stick it in me," Dan said. Lance was amazed that Al was shoving his fuck stick up Dan's butt. He didn't think Dan would be the type of guy to get fucked up the ass. Then he started to feel Dan's shaft massage his bowels. Reaching between his legs, he grabbed hold of his cock. Precum oozed out from the tip and puddled on the ground.

"That feels good," Dan said, slamming his meat in and out of Lance's body. Lance agreed. Getting fucked up the ass felt even better than he'd imagined it would. It was nothing like having his fingers do the work, it was so much better. Especially having Dan's thick dick stretching his hole. Lance felt Dan's cock head swell up his ass as he stroked himself.

Lance was so close to getting off. He let go of his dick and pulled down on his balls.

Dan's rod kept moving up his fuck chute. Grabbing his cock again, he moved his hand over the swollen head.

"Fuck," Dan called out as his knob pulsed up Lance's hot hole. "I'm coming."

That was when Lance nearly lost balance and shot his load on the ground in pulsing blasts.

Dan pulled his cock out of Lance's ass. Stepping away from

Dan, Lance watched Al still hard at work fucking Dan. Al grabbed Dan's hips, slammed his fuck stick in good and hard, then pulled back. Then Al let out a grunt. His body shuddered. Al pulled back, then slammed in again, then he jabbed at Dan's fuck hole with short, quick prods as he came up his ass.

Lance pulled up his jeans and buttoned them as Al pulled his cock out of Dan's asshole. "How about the three of us head inside?" Lance said.

Al held up the used condom. "Sure, I need to get rid of this."

"And we can relax a bit, maybe go for another round," Lance said.

Dan grinned. "I'm game," he said.

Lance was game, too.

TROUBLE AT MILKWOOD FARMS

Dennis Jacobs pulled the black, two door Ford Explorer into the parking lot of the quickie mart, then checked out his hair one more time. It was true, he needed to get his hair cut once he was finished with the interview. After making sure the dark tips of hair were tucked behind his ears, he got out of the car. Dennis brushed nonexistent lint off his white shirt, then fixed the knot in his tie as he walked towards the glass paneled store front.

Dennis pulled the glass door open, scanned the floor, then the aisles. Everything appeared in order, no dust on the shelves and the floors were clean. Sean, one of the newest hires, was behind the cash register, his navy blue smock unwrinkled, his name tag in perfect view. Dennis couldn't help but notice how well Sean's clothes clung to his athletic form, and the way his brown eyes invited a second look. Hopefully those same eyes would lure shoppers back into the store for another peek, and perhaps an extra half gallon of milk. If Sean wasn't one of Dennis's employees, he would come back for a second look, and maybe even try to score the guy.

"Bob's in the back," Sean said.

Dennis strolled into the back room. Sitting in front of a makeshift desk that consisted of a door lying across two saw horses was Bob, the store manager, sitting on some milk crates stacked next to the far wall. Standing up, Bob scratched his big belly. Bob wore the navy blue lacrosse shirt with the company logo. "He's in the bathroom," Bob said, pointing to the door to the left of the cooler door.

The toilet flushed, then the door opened. Dennis glanced down at the desk and scanned the application. Jake Polgram, age eighteen.

"This is Jake," Bob said.

Dennis looked up, then saw the young man. Nowhere on the application did it mention his well defined jaw, dark eyes and full lips. Nor was his firm body beneath the tight t-shirt brought up, or the massive bulge of eager cock between his legs. Dennis's prick began to react as he held out his hand and gave Jake a firm shake. Jake smiled. Even his teeth were perfect. For a moment he considered asking Bob to stay, but that would be unusual.

"Well," Bob said, "I'll be out front if you need me."

Bob walked out, leaving Dennis alone with Jake in the small, dimly lit room with the cement floor. Grabbing Jake's application, Dennis glanced through it one more time. When he looked up, he noticed Jake's hand dangling between his open legs, and the thick outline of cock running down his right thigh. His big balls seemed ready to break through the thick cotton material. Dennis knew he couldn't deal with walking into the store and seeing Jake behind the counter every time he checked in on store 2057 and collected the payroll and inventory. If he hired this boy, he was going to be in trouble.

"So, you looking for part time?" Dennis said, shifting in his seat to ease the pressure building between his legs.

"Yes," Jake said.

Dennis studied the application. He was going off to college, full time. Well, the store needed someone who could stay past the summer. "You're going to college."

"Yes, Providence College. Local boy, local school. Plus my dad went there, so he's real proud to have me going, too." Jake rubbed his upper thighs, the thumb of his right hand almost touching his meat.

"Can you work here and not have it interfere with school?"

"I don't see why not," Jake said. He leaned back and placed his hands behind his head, then stretched his long legs. "I did it all through high school and made honors."

"Honors." Dennis looked down at the application. His cock was so hard that he knew he wouldn't be able to stand by the end of the interview. The cocky fuck had made honors and worked part time at Dingo Mart, which was on the opposite side of the city.

"Dingo Mart," Jake said.

"I see. It's right here." Dennis was losing control of the interview. He couldn't let that happen. "What made you leave your last job?"

"This place is closer to school."

"But you'll be living at home, I assume."

"I'm a big boy, Mr. Jacobs."

That was an understatement. "And where will you be living?"

"The dorms."

There was a checkmark in the upper right hand corner of the application. Bob wanted to hire this kid. Dennis couldn't find any reason not to hire him, other than the fact that he wouldn't be able to visit the store and keep his concentration if Jake was around. If it was up to him, he wouldn't hire him. But if he didn't, then he would have to explain why he didn't want the kid working there. Bob wouldn't understand.

"Is something wrong?" Jake asked.

"No," Dennis said. "When can you start?"

"When do you want me?"

A thousand lines shot through Dennis's head, and not a single one of them was appropriate.

Dennis hoped there wouldn't be any problems once he was used to Jake being around. He tugged on his hairy nuts, feeling the fleshy sack in his grip, then slipped into bed, feeling the soft cotton sheets against his skin. His cock was stiff, rising up thick and stiff, the tip moist with precum. Grabbing the spare pillow, he shoved it under the covers and slipped it between his legs. His cock and balls pushed into the smooth softness of the pillow, rubbing against it with each inward movement of his hips.

Jake was hot, there was no way around it. Dennis could still see Jake clear as day, sitting with his legs outstretched, his cock and balls running down his thigh. The ever so secure look on his handsome face. And those lips, so full. How nice they would look with his cock stuffed between them. Surely the boy liked to suck dick. Just one look at him and it was easy to imagine that he'd be a pro at it. A mouth like that was made to suck dick. Then there was his ass, so perfectly round and firm. Fuckable, that's what it was.

Dennis grabbed the head of his long, thin prick and rubbed it, feeling the precum against his palm. He would love to fuck Jake's ass. The hole had to be tight. He imagined Jake's fuck hole kissing the head of his dick, then opening up to swallow the length. Dennis would give it to him too. He'd fuck that little college boy until he screamed for more.

Gripping the shaft, he started to stroke it while imagining leaning against the front register, wearing nothing but the navy blue store apron, his bare ass exposed and waiting for Dennis to stick his prick inside. Then he imagined Jake looking back at him, that know-it-all grin on his face. "You want to fuck me, don't you?" Jake whispered.

Not only that, but Dennis also wanted to lick his ass. What he wouldn't do for the chance to get down and tickle the boy's pucker with the tip of his tongue. Lick it good, get it good and wet. How nice it would be to have Jake's ass cheeks on either side of his face as he licked his pucker.

Dennis was getting himself worked up to a froth, but he couldn't stop stroking. Then his legs tightened, and he shot his creamy load.

Dennis was on the road, heading to store 2286 when his beeper went off. Pulling the small black beeper off his belt, he looked at the thin LCD screen on top. He had one quick stop before the end of the day, and now his beeper had to go off. It was one of the stores, that much he knew. Then it hit him, it wasn't just any store, it was store 2057. Dennis tossed the beeper onto the passenger seat, then his hand flew to the cellular phone. With one hand on the steering wheel, and brief glimpses towards the outstretched highway, Dennis was able to dial store 2057. It rang once. Again. Someone had to be there. One more ring. Come on.

"Milkwood Farms Convenience Store." It was Bob, sounding a little odd, as if in pain.

"Bob, what's going on?" Dennis asked.

"Dennis, I hate to bother you, but I need some help," Bob said. "I broke my finger."

"You what?" Dennis couldn't believe what he was hearing.

"I can't find anyone to come in," Bob said.

"Lock up."

"I can't." There was commotion in the background, then the whir of the lottery machine.

"Can you get to a hospital?"

"Blake is coming by." Blake was Bob's roommate.

Dennis could call store 2286 on the way to 2057, and reschedule the meeting with the manager for the next day. "I'll be there."

"I'm sorry about this."

Dennis hung up the phone, then veered off the highway. Once Dennis was off the highway, he picked up the cell phone and dialed store 2286. It was going to be a late night.

When Dennis got to the store, Bob had already left. Jake was behind the register, ringing up a last customer. It was Tuesday, Jake's first day on the job. "Where's Bob?" Dennis asked. "He had to go to the hospital, I thought you knew," Jake said. "He left you alone?"

"He told me to stay at the register, and that you would be here soon. It's not like I've never worked a register before."

"How are you doing with the lottery?"

"Okay," Jake said. "Bob wouldn't have left me alone if he didn't think I could do it."

Jake was right. It wasn't as if Bob was irresponsible. Stepping behind the counter, Dennis caught a glimpse of Jake's firm, rounded ass. Luckily the navy blue apron was covering the front of Jake's body, although there was a slight protrusion where his cock and balls were held tight in the thick jean material.

"Is there anything you would like to show me?" Jake asked, his full lips forming the perfect grin.

"Just stay at the register," Dennis said, turning towards the counter to hide his growing erection. "I'm just going to do some paper work until it's time to close. I'll show you how to close out the register."

"Sure," Jake said.

Dennis went out to the Ford Explorer and grabbed his briefcase. He did have enough paper work to keep himself occupied, but kept sneaking glances at Jake's firm body anyway. Every now and again Jake would press his hands against the counter top, lean forward and stretch. His ass looked so damn hot protruding out. Dennis couldn't hold back the images of tickling Jake's asshole with the tip of his tongue. There were even a few times when he'd considered what it would taste like to suck Jake's big dick. How big was it, exactly? To form such a nice lump that was slightly visible behind the apron, it had to be at least seven inches, and thick. He probably had nice big balls, too. Dennis tried to remind himself that Jake was an employee, but that didn't do any good. Not even the sound of the cash register drawer opening and closing, or the churning of the lottery ticket machine was enough to take Dennis's mind off Jake's body.

Dennis hoped Bob might come back, although he doubted that was a possibility. As the hours ticked by, and Dennis faked doing his paper work, it had become even more evident that Bob wasn't going to be coming back, and Dennis would have to close up the store alone with Jake.

"Well, it's time to close up," Jake said, lifting his arms in the air and stretching. He pushed his hand into the pocket of his jeans and produced his keys. "Bob already gave me a copy of the key to the store." Then he walked towards Dennis, brushing past him as he walked out from behind the counter.

Dennis packed the papers back into his briefcase, then set it aside. Jake's apron was off, and the buttons keeping the fly of his jeans closed were bulging.

"Are you okay?" Jake asked.

"Let's get you cashed out," Dennis said, then turned towards the cash register and ran the X and Y reports. After that he explained how to Z the register out, and the both of them counted up the drawer. Dennis let Jake fill out the paper work as he explained where the numbers were put on the sheet, then which to add and which to subtract. He tried not to stand too close to Jake, but every time he moved to the side, it seemed that Jake moved closer.

Behind the register, set into the floor, was the drop safe. Jake stood as Dennis squatted down and opened the safe and stuck the money and paper work inside. He looked up at Jake, past the boy's ample basket and tried not to drool. The back of Jake's hand brushed over the bulge of cock and balls, and Dennis wasn't sure how obvious his erection would be if he stood. But he couldn't stay down there all night, so he had no choice.

Taking hold of Dennis's waist, Jake moved behind him. "I'm going to get the mop ready to wash the floor," he said. "Can you show me where everything is in the back room?"

Dennis followed Jake into the back room, and was about to tell him not to bother with the floor when he saw Jake at the sink attaching the hose to the faucet. The yellow bucket that was on casters was in front of the sink, the mop leaning against the wall to the left of Jake.

"You look stressed," Jake said, turning to look at Dennis. He held the hose at crotch level and filled the yellow bucket with water.

"No, I'm fine," Dennis said, trying to keep his eyes away from Jake's bulging crotch. It was already too late to hide his own hardon, which he knew was obvious. "Maybe I should go and put my briefcase in the car."

"Afraid to get dirty?" Jake said. He turned the water off, then dropped the hose in the sink.

Dennis grinned. "No, I'm not."

"Then loosen your tie and relax." Jake leaned back against the edge of the sink and spread his legs. He glanced at Dennis's basket. "You look like you need to relax a little."

Dennis swallowed. Jake was flirting with him. Between Jake's comment, and the way he looked at Dennis's crotch, it was too obvious to be mistaken for anything else. He couldn't act on it, though. It wasn't professional.

Jake grabbed his crotch. "You've been looking at it all night," he said, slowly unbuttoning the fly.

Jake was going to show him his dick. Dennis watched in awe as Jake pulled out his thick, eight inches and waved it at him. The head was ripe, precum dripping from the piss slit. A purple vein ran along the length of the shaft. Reaching into the fly of his jeans once more, Jake pulled out his big hairy nuts, which hung loose in their sack below the massive rod.

Dennis walked up to Jake, reached out and gripped Jake's thick shaft, feeling it firm up in his hand. He'd been wanting to touch the boy's prick for so long, and now he was doing it. Then Jake's hand unzipped Dennis's fly, pulled down his BVDs and gripped his shaft.

Jake kissed Dennis. Their lips parted and Dennis sucked on Jake's tongue. Jake took his hand off Dennis's cock, then placed his hands on Dennis's shoulders. Their lips parted, and Dennis went down on his knees. Jake's prick was in front of him, the head bobbing inches from his lips. Dennis parted his lips and felt the head fill his mouth, then gently glide over his tongue. It filled his throat as Jake moved his hips forward, shoving the entire shaft into Dennis's mouth, and down his throat. Reaching up, Dennis grabbed Jake's big balls and gave them a gentle tug. He bobbed his head, taking the meaty shaft down his throat, feeling the meaty knob pushing out against the inside of his gullet. Slag formed around his mouth and dripped onto the floor.

While the cock was buried down his throat, Dennis reached up and unbuttoned the top button of Jake's jeans, then pulled them down. He slid the shaft out of his mouth, allowing it to bob in front of him, then slipped his hand between Jake's legs, gliding his fingers along the thin seam of flesh that went from his balls to his tight asshole. Jake parted his legs as Dennis pressed his middle finger against the tight pucker.

"Turn around," Dennis said.

Jake turned, then leaned against the sink. Jake's ass was smooth, with tight round cheeks. Dennis parted the fleshy mounds, exposing the boy's pucker. The sweet smell of ass filled his nostrils as he ducked his head between the crack and gave the hole a lick with the flat of his tongue. Moving back, he saw the hole wink at him. What Dennis wanted was to stick his dick inside that tight little fuck hole. He wanted to feel it grip his prick, caress it until he blew his load. Spreading his ass cheeks again, Dennis pushed both thumbs against the pucker, and watched it open. He pushed his thumbs inside, slowly moving them in and out of the hole. Jake's ass was so tight. Dennis's dick began to twitch.

"I have a condom in my pocket," Jake said.

Dennis searched Jake's jeans, finding the condom in his left pocket. He unrolled the latex sheath over his prick, then spit on Jake's hole. Standing up, he slapped his prick against the tight opening a few times, then pushed the head against it. The sphincter opened up and gripped the head. Slowly, Dennis pushed more of his prick inside, feeling the warmth and smoothness of Jake's fuck chute.

"You feel good," Jake said once Dennis's entire rod was buried deep within his bowels. "I've been wanting you to fuck me since my interview."

Dennis pulled his shaft back until only the head was inside, then pushed it back inside. "You're so fucking tight," he said. Dennis held onto Jake's hips, then shoved his shaft back inside, then pulled out and went back in. He got a good rhythm going as he fucked Jake's ass, feeling the hot spunk fill his prick.

Jake started stroking his meat, forcing his balls to swing back with each downward thrust. Feeling Jake's balls come close to his crotch drove Dennis wild. He slammed his prick in quick, causing Jake to let out a soft moan.

"Yeah, man, fuck me," Jake said softly.

So Dennis started fucking his ass harder. He knew it wasn't going to be long before he came. He slammed in hard again, pulled back and shoved it back in. The muscles in Dennis's legs began to tighten, his breathing became heavy. The head of his cock was ripe and eager to blow.

"Fucking give it to me, man," Jake said.

And that's just what Dennis did. Letting out a deep groan, he felt the head of his cock pulse, then he shot his load. His pace slowed as he emptied his ball juice up Jake's ass, then pulled out when he'd finished.

Dennis's prick was still hard as it came out of Jake's fuck hole. He peeled off the condom, then tossed it in an empty box near the opposite wall. He'd have to remember to throw that box away before he left.

"Come down here and suck my dick," Jake said. "It's my turn."

Once again Dennis found himself on his knees, feeling Jake's massive prick poking at the back of his throat. He sucked it down, swallowing every last inch until his nose was pushing into Jake's pubic hair.

"Suck my big dick," Jake said, holding onto Dennis's head as it bobbed up and down on his prod.

Then Jake's cock head plumped up even more in Dennis's throat, and he had to take it out of his mouth. Spit drooled from Dennis's lips as the moist shaft shot up in front of him. Jake gripped his shaft and gave it a few strokes. Jake let out a deep groan. Dennis leaned back, and watched as the first thick load of creamy fuck juice shot out of Jake's piss slit and hit the floor. The second shot landed on the yellow bucket, and the third fell just short of the bucket. The rest of his load fell to the floor at Jake's feet as he slowed his pace.

Dennis stood up, straightened his pants, then brushed off his knees. "I guess you can mop up now," he said.

Jake shook his head. "You still sorry you hired me?"

Dennis shook his head, then walked out of the back room. Maybe Jake would work out after all.

THE BOYS OF DEL SOL ADVERTISING

From the moment Mitch Cantrel walked into the offices of Del Sol Advertising Alan knew he was in trouble. Fixing the poster boards for his latest proposal Alan spied Mitch walking out of Bruce Montano's office with an award winning grin and cocky stride. Mitch's dark suit fit him perfectly, accenting his broad shoulders and beautiful green eyes. Turning towards Alan, Mitch waved and said hello in a deep, friendly tone. Alan waved back, and knew that Mitch had everything Bruce Montano wanted in all of his advertising men, right down to his dark, short cropped hair style. Alan wasn't afraid Mitch would steal his job, he'd been with the company for over five years, had won over too many big money contracts, and had kept himself looking neat and in shape. No, it wasn't lack of job security that made Alan feel Mitch Cantrel was trouble, it was the feeling he got between his legs when Mitch walked by. Alan never slept with anyone that was his equal in the company; it made things complicated, and wasn't good for business.

Alan turned towards his campaign board. There was the photograph of the handsome, older man with the dark chest hair, and firm stomach standing legs akimbo with his arms crossed, wearing nothing but a white ribbed jock strap. Below the model, in simple bold print was: Everything you want in a jock. And judging by the bulge in the model's crotch, he did have everything any healthy, modern man would want.

A firm hand clasped Alan's shoulder. "Well, let's see that ad campaign before they get here," Bruce Montano said. Bruce walked up to the advertisement, and all Alan could see of him was the back of his gray head. Bruce wasn't wearing a jacket, and even in a white cotton shirt and deep blue slacks, his v-shaped torso and firm ass were evident. Alan wished he would look as good when he hit fifty.

"What do you think?" Alan asked.

Bruce turned, rubbing his chin with a well manicured hand. "Brilliant. What's the rest of the campaign like?"

"I used the same model, but changed the slogan a little," Alan said. "The model is in different positions, of course."

"I can't wait to see the presentation." Bruce turned away from the advertisement. "Did you see the young man who stepped out of my office?"

Alan nodded as his cock stirred from the mere thought of the man Bruce was talking about.

"That's Mitch Cantrel. I want you to work on the Slessinger campaign with him," Bruce said. "He'll be meeting you here first thing Monday morning. I want you to show him everything you know."

"But I was hoping to come in over the weekend to start working on that campaign," Alan said.

"Well then, you'll just have to give Mitch a call and see if he wants to join you over the weekend. I'll have my secretary give you his phone number."

By the end of the work day Alan was tired and horny. Bruce still hadn't sent his secretary over with Mitch's phone number, and Alan hoped he'd forgotten, although Bruce Montano never forgot anything.

"Excuse me, Mr. Olin," David, Bruce's young secretary, said as he stood with his arms crossed. Being Friday, David was allowed to dress down, and his tight jeans did an excellent job of showing off the large slab of boy meat between his legs. He clutched a small piece of paper in his left hand.

"Come in, David," Alan said, adjusting his tie.

"Mr. Montano wanted me to give you Mr. Cantrel's phone number." David walked in front of Alan's desk and held out the phone number.

Alan couldn't help but think how nice David's full lips would look with his big, thick cock stuffed between them. He took the paper, and winked at David. David's blue eyes sparkled in response.

There was a knock at the door, and Bruce popped his head inside. "I'm off for the day," Bruce said. "David, lock the office up before you leave."

"Will do, Mr. Montano," David said.

Alan slid Mitch's phone number to the left of his typed notes for the Slessinger campaign. "David, could you also do me a favor before you leave?"

"Anything you want," David said.

Alan held out the notes. "Can you make a copy of these for me? I need them to give to Mitch."

"Will do," David said.

Alan had gotten off the phone with Mitch Cantrel, and the boner in his pants hadn't gone down. Listening to Mitch's deep voice hadn't helped matters any. Unzipping his slacks, Alan pulled his hard cock out of the opening in his boxer shorts and wiped the precum off the piss slit with his index finger. He licked his finger clean, then brought his hand back down to give the shaft a stroke.

"I have those copies, Mr. Olin," David said, walking around the desk.

Alan tried to keep his chair rolled in so David wouldn't see his cock. He held out his hand, but not in time to prevent the sheets from falling to the floor. The chair rolled away from the desk from Alan's initial response to catch the falling papers, but David was already kneeling down next to him, gathering the sheets that had slipped under the desk.

"Can you move your foot, Mr. Olin?" David asked.

Hesitantly, Alan rolled his chair back, and moved his leg. He looked down, and caught David trying not to look at his stiff dick.

"I didn't mean to disturb you," David said, handing the papers to Alan. "Is there anything else you would like me to do for you, sir?"

Alan looked down at David, and watched the boy lick his lips. "There is one thing I would like," Alan said.

David reached out and took Alan's shaft in his hand, then wrapped his lips around the bulbous head and sucked the entire eight inch shaft down his hungry throat. Then he popped the stiff meat out of his mouth. "Is that okay, Mr. Olin?"

"Very much so." Alan took off his tie and unbuttoned his shirt, exposing his smooth chest, then scooted his ass to the edge of the chair. Leaning back, he watched the handsome boy suck his cock. David's throat was warm and moist, and his gullet caressed his shaft and brought him close to the edge of coming. Then David pulled the massive cock out of his mouth, and licked around the ripe head. David tickled the heart shaped underside with the tip of his tongue, and Alan felt his legs tighten.

"I'm going to shoot soon," Alan said.

David gave Alan's prick a few quick tugs. It was more than Alan could take. His body tightened, then he shot his load in pulsing spurts that covered his stomach and chest with creamy drops of spunk.

Grabbing hold of his meat, Alan slapped it against David's mouth. "What about you?" Alan asked as he grabbed a cum towel out of the bottom drawer of his desk.

"What about me?" David asked playfully.

Wiping the cum off himself, Alan asked, "Don't you want to get off, too?"

Standing up, David rubbed the large, protruding bulge in his jeans. "Why don't I close that door?"

"Go ahead," Alan said, then watched David's round ass move as he walked to the door, then turned.

Leaning against the door, David unbuttoned the fly of his jeans and pulled out his seven inch hardon, then lobbed out his big, hairy balls. He slowly stroked his shaft as he walked back to the desk and held his dick in front of Alan's face.

Alan swallowed David's prick, feeling it fill his mouth as he sucked and drank up the precum that drooled out of the slit. David grabbed a lock of Alan's hair, then force fed him his shaft until the head swelled and was ready to burst.

David stepped back, and his shaft popped out of Alan's mouth. Giving his rod a few quick strokes, David cupped his hand in front of the swollen knob. Then David let out a groan, and hot spunk drooled out of the tip of his prick and filled his palm with milky white jizm. When he was finished coming, he licked his palm clean.

"Will that be all, Mr. Olin?" David asked.

"Yes, that will do." Alan leaned back in his chair and patted his stomach. It was too bad David wasn't going to be around Saturday; he might need a boy like him by the end of the day.

Naked, Alan sat in his bedroom window, toes pressed against the inside of the window frame, and looked out. Eight flights below was the busy city street, with people scurrying along, never looking up. The window was his favorite place to sit and think, not to mention the many times he'd sat there and pulled his pud.

Nobody ever looked up, and even if they did they wouldn't be able to make out what he was doing. Across the street was a business office, and all the lights were off.

The Slessinger campaign was big money, the last thing he needed was to have to explain everything to some new guy who might have his own ideas about advertising. And to top all that off, Mitch was fucking hot. Alan didn't need his mind to be wandering off on Mitch's body when it should be busy thinking about the campaign. As it was his cock was already stiff just from thinking about working with Mitch.

Alan grabbed his shaft and gave it a stroke. Then he noticed some movement in the office window across the street. There was a light on in the office; it wasn't direct, but it was enough for him to see a man standing in the window with his cock hanging out of a one piece uniform. Whoever it was was stroking his shaft. Alan lowered his leg so the guy could get a good view of his meat, and saw the man nod. Slowly, Alan continued to stroke his cock with the man across the street. If they could see each other, then anyone in that building on the same floor could probably see him. The mere thought made Alan even more excited. The man across the street was still stroking his meat, then his body jolted and he sprayed hot cream all over the window. Alan watched as the man's jizm streaked the glass.

That was all it took for Alan to feel his legs tighten, then he let out a grunt and shot his load.

It was Saturday, so Alan didn't bother getting dressed up in a suit and tie for the office. Instead he wore jeans, running shoes and an old, stretched out t-shirt. The office was empty, so Alan decided to take the time to go and make some coffee.

When he stepped out of the office, he heard the familiar sound of coffee being brewed, then took in the rich scent. He peered down the hall and saw Mitch Cantrel, dressed in a pair of dark blue sweat pants, a mustard t-shirt, and sneakers, taking two mugs out of the overhead cabinet.

"Hey there," Mitch said, walking up to Alan to shake his hand. That was when Alan noticed the pale ring around Mitch's left ring finger. Either Mitch was divorced or he'd taken his wedding ring off for some reason.

"Making coffee," Alan said as he pulled his hand out of Mitch's firm grip.

"I haven't had a cup yet," Mitch said, then smiled.

"I could use a cup, too," Alan said.

Flashing his award winning smile, Mitch said, "It's going to be great working with you."

"Well, I have some notes on the campaign for you on my desk."

"That's great. I've seen your work before, when I worked at Croft and Sonengrass."

"Aren't they in L.A.?" Alan asked.

"Yes, they are." Mitch turned and his big, meaty cock lobbed around in his sweat pants. "After the divorce, I figured it might be a good idea to get away from everything, so I decided to move east."

"I'm sorry."

"Hey, I'm working for one of the best advertising companies on the east coast, and with a guy whose work I've always admired." Mitch shrugged, and raised his eyebrows. "You can't beat that."

"Hey, look, why don't you go into the office and look over the notes. I'll bring the coffee in when it's done," Alan said. "Do you take cream?"

"Lots of cream, no sugar," Mitch said before walking away. Alan watched Mitch's firm, round ass move in his sweats. Alan couldn't believe any woman would dump a man like Mitch Cantrel. What was that woman thinking?

The final bursts of steam escaped the coffee maker, and Alan's cock was already begging for attention. Alan adjusted his meat, hoping it would go down before he got back to the office. Mitch was a straight, divorced man, he kept telling himself as he poured the coffee into the cups, then fixed them up with cream.

Mitch was looking at the jock strap advertisement that was still set up across from the desk when Alan walked in, coffee in hand. Mitch's thick dick looked to be at half mast. The head was outlined in the cloth and hung a good seven inches. Alan handed Mitch the coffee.

"That's a great ad," Mitch said.

"Thanks." Alan knew he should have never moved the boards back into his office after the meeting the previous night. Now they were going to be a big distraction. "I was thinking maybe we should move this into the conference room." It was a good idea, and made sense. "We'll have more space to work."

"Sounds good to me," Mitch said.

After grabbing both sets of notes from his desk, Alan escorted Mitch to the conference room. The long mahogany table and cushioned chairs looked inviting. There were some pens and pencils at the end of the desk.

"So, what are we selling?" Mitch asked, taking a seat on top of the conference table, legs spread, cock and balls bulging through the cotton sweats.

"Cologne." Alan placed his hands firmly on the back of the chair to the right of Mitch. He had to keep his mind on work and off Mitch's bulging crotch.

"Women's or men's?"

"Men's. It's called Instinct," Alan said. He couldn't step away from the chair now, his cock would be too noticeable. "The idea I want to get across is that a guy isn't dressed unless he's wearing Instinct. We're marketing this to older, professional men. What we want is a model with a well defined, hairy chest. Someone handsome, but not too handsome."

Mitch slid his hand under his shirt, lifting the bottom up enough for Alan to see the thin line of hair leading into his sweat pants, and scratched his side. "And how is he dressed?" Mitch asked.

"Well, that's the catch," Alan said, looking into Mitch's green eyes. "He isn't dressed. And the caption is, Now I'm ready for anything."

"I like it," Mitch said, resting his left hand on his thigh so his fingers crossed his shaft. "Sounds like you have print covered, what about commercial?"

"I have no idea." Alan's cock wasn't going down. He shifted his stance, and the long tube of flesh rubbed against the inside of his jeans. He tried to remind himself that Mitch was a straight boy. The band of white flesh on his ring finger testified to that.

"How about this?" Mitch leapt off the desk, his cock and balls swinging back and forth from the movement, then stood in front of the doorway. "A bedroom. Soft lighting. A man rises from bed in a t-shirt and boxer shorts. He pulls off his shirt." Mitch lifted his t-shirt over his head, exposing his well sculpted torso, and the thick hair on his pectorals that narrowed into a thin line leading to his crotch. "He walks into the bathroom, takes off his boxers, then steps into the shower." Mitch walked up to Alan, his cock rising up higher in his sweats. "And when he comes out of the shower, he puts on the cologne. Fade out. Black screen. White letters that say, Now he's ready for anything."

Alan couldn't speak. His cock was aching for attention, and Mitch was standing shirtless in front of him. He reached out and buried his hand in the thick hair on Mitch's chest. Alan *was* ready for anything.

Mitch leaned forward and kissed Alan. Their mouths opened, and Mitch darted his tongue into Alan's mouth. Then Mitch's hands were inside Alan's t-shirt, lifting it up and over his head. The two men wrapped their arms around each other, feeling their torsos. It wasn't long before Alan slid his hands inside Mitch's sweat pants and pulled them down.

Mitch was horse hung. His cut cock bounced at half mast, pre-cum dripping off the knobby head. Alan gripped the shaft, then swallowed it in one hungry gulp. "Oh fuck, yes," Mitch said through clenched teeth. "That's good. That is so fucking good."

Alan stopped sucking Mitch's shaft, and started licking his hairy, low hanging balls. He sucked them in his mouth and closed his lips. Then he popped them out of his mouth and Mitch let out a sigh.

"Come up here," Mitch said.

Alan rose to his feet. Mitch unbuttoned Alan's jeans as Alan kicked off his running shoes. Soon both men were naked. Mitch lifted Alan and sat him down on the conference table. Grabbing Alan's ankles, he lifted his legs in the air and kissed his pucker. He gave the tight hole a lick, then started working on Alan's big nuts. It felt so good that Alan thought he was going to blow his load. How in the world could a straight boy be so eager to lick his ass and balls? It wasn't until Mitch started sucking his cock head that Alan no longer gave Mitch's sexuality another thought.

Mitch slid it in and out of his throat like a pro. Resting on his elbows, Alan watched Mitch work his shaft, feeling his hot throat engulf his cock, bringing him close to orgasm. But he didn't want to cum yet, so he reached out and pulled Mitch's face away from his prick.

"What's wrong?" Mitch asked.

"I don't want to cum yet," Alan said.

"I want to see you cum." Mitch gently ran the tips of his fingers over the length of Alan's shaft.

"For a straight man, you really know how to turn a guy on," Alan said.

"Who said I was straight?" Mitch kissed the inside of Alan's thigh.

"You're not?"

"No. I wanted to be, at one time." Mitch climbed up on the table and stretched out next to Alan. He stroked Alan's chest, then gently held Alan's hard shaft. "That's why I got divorced. I couldn't deny my feelings for men's bodies."

Alan took Mitch's dick in his hand and stroked it. Soon Mitch's breathing was hard and fast, then he let out a groan, his body jerked, and he shot globs of hot spunk all over Alan's chest and stomach.

Mitch kissed Alan. "It's your turn," he said, then took hold of Alan's cock, close to the head, and gave it a few quick jerks.

That was all it took to get Alan off. Blast after blast of thick jizm spurted from his cock, the first hitting his throat, the other shots landing on his chest, mixing with Mitch's cum puddles.

"Maybe we should work together more often," Alan said, stroking Mitch's back.

"First let's get you cleaned off." Mitch slid off the table and stepped into his sweat pants. "Where can I find a towel?"

"Probably under the sink." Alan relaxed as Mitch stepped out. He liked Mitch's idea for the commercial, it definitely sold him.

IT COULD HAPPEN TO YOU

There really isn't anything special about the way I look. I'm not saying that I'm ugly, just that there is nothing outstanding about my appearance. Like most guys who care about how they look, I keep in shape. My body is toned, but there isn't anything about me that sets me apart from the rest of the crowd. I'm not putting myself down, just being honest. When I look at myself in the mirror I see an average looking man with a normal build. When I say normal, I mean everything about me is normal. My legs, chest, hands, feet, dick are all of normal proportion. Oh, since I'm running down a list of body parts, let's not forget my balls, which are not too large nor do they hang exceedingly low.

To get off the subject of my body I would have to say there is nothing odd or different about my daily routine either. My days start out just like every other guy's, with a boner and a cup of coffee. After that I shower, shave and get dressed for a day at the office. And sure, like most guys I sometimes jerk off in the shower. Hey, it's normal. All guys do it. I mean, you're soaping up your nuts, practically playing with yourself already, so why not just grab hold of your pole and give it a few srokes? Thousands of men do it all over the country every morning. There is nothing special about it. And so, after a jerk off session in the shower, I get dressed and head for work.

My job, like everything else about me, is nothing special. I work in an office like a lot of other guys, taking on projects for my boss and staying in my cramped office for more than eight hours every day trying to get as much accomplished as possible. I ride the same subway train into work every day, but do not usually take the same train home. Like I said, my day does not end after eight hours, but when I feel I'm caught up enough to call it a day. You must be getting eager for me to get to the story, so now with all of this said I can begin to tell you my juicy story.

The day I'm going to tell you about began like any normal day, with me taking the subway. The subway train I take into work can get rather cramped, which means I often have to stand and grab hold of the overhead railing so I don't topple into anyone standing close to me. So on any given morning you can find me crammed into a subway car with no place to look but straight ahead. Most days there isn't anything to look at except for the advertisements plastered in a row near the roof of the train, but every now and again I'm standing close to this punky looking guy with a tight body, close cut head of hair, round glasses and dirty smirk on his face. His glasses are not tinted or anything, which leads me to believe they are prescription. I've seen this man many times before, and he is someone you cannot forget.

Every time I saw him on the train prior to this day that I'm telling you about I would feel my dick begin to stiffen. In fact, I would get so concerned about my bulging prick that I would have to make sure not to look at him too long. And the few times he'd caught me looking at him he would give me this smart ass sneer that would make me wonder if he was planning on picking my pocket before he got together with one of his pals to rob a bank or go car jacking. In fact, there was one day when he was standing so close to me that I could have held his hand. I grabbed hold of the pole behind me for support while he grabbed hold of the overhead bar and let his left hand dangle next to my body. Every time the subway car swayed from side to side his wrist would brush against my stiffening prick. At one point he turned towards me, looked me up and down and smirked. I tried to act casual. I even smiled and said hello. He didn't say a word, just rubbed the back of his hand against my prick, then got off at the next stop.

When I arrived at work that day, the day he rubbed my crotch, my prick was begging for attention. In fact, my dick was so stiff that I had to walk into work with my briefcase in front of me to hide what was obviously stated between my legs. And once behind the safety of my desk, out came my prick. Eyes closed, I imagined that the guy from the train walked into my office to ask if I'm queer. Not only that, let me tell you, he walked into the office without a shirt on so I could see the sweat gleaming off his well developed chest. Oh yes, I was in my glory as I sat there imagining this and stroking my cock. Then he walked behind my desk, placed his bulging crotch in my face and asked me again if I'm queer. I didn't say anything, just looked up at him as he unbuttoned his fly and lugged out his thick slab of meat. "I think you are," he said, then slapped me in the face with his cock. I watched as his prick became hard. He jabbed the head of his prick at me, forcing me to open my mouth and suck on the knob. That's when he slammed his meat down my throat and started fucking my face real hard. The guy rode my mouth like a cowboy taking a bull. I could feel his cock head down my throat, plumping up, getting ready to blow a load of hot spunk. Then he pulled his shaft out of my throat and slapped his wet tube of flesh against my face before giving it a few strokes. Cum splashed against my cheeks in pulsing blasts. I felt myself about to cum and cupped my free hand over the head and felt hot jizm squirting into my palm. When I was finished coming I looked around my office, and for the first time admitted that I wanted to suck that guy's cock.

And so, as you can probably guess, this guy, this nameless guy was the object of my lust. Every time I jerked off it was while picturing him making me do things. He'd tell me to bend over and spread my ass cheeks so he could fuck me good and hard, or have me lick his hairy nuts or suck his cock. And as time went on I would see him, the very guy I'd jerked off thinking about while in the shower, standing on the opposite side of the subway car looking at me with that cocky grin. There were a few times—usually on the days I didn't have time to jerk off in the shower—that I would hope he would stand next to me and rub his hand against my crotch once more, but for some reason that didn't happen again.

Now, to get back to the story at hand, there I was in the subway at ten o'clock at night after putting in a full day at the office. It was August, and the subways were dank and heavy with summer air and I was thankful that the train would be air-conditioned. I was alone at the subway stop, which made me stay on my guard. I had heard stories of people being mugged while waiting alone for the train and I didn't want to become one of those unfortunate people. It wasn't until the train could be heard roaring through the tunnel that I was able to breathe a sigh of relief.

Someone's heavy footsteps running down the train platform rang through the subway tunnel as the doors to the train slid open. It was him, the tough little punk that I'd jerked off thinking about countless times. He jumped through the doorway behind me, grabbed the pole rising up from the floor and joining the ceiling and swung himself into a seat. I sat across from him, watching as he pulled off his t-shirt to wipe some sweat off his face and out from under his armpits. He wore sneakers with no socks and baggy, plaid shorts. I watched his muscular calves as he spread his legs apart and scratched his crotch, his balls and shaft moving beneath the fabric with the motion of his fingers. He looked at me, sneered, then pushed his head up in some form of hello. He rubbed his thigh.

Now let me tell you, it is a very odd feeling that runs through you when you find yourself alone with the object of your lust sneering at you this way. I was concerned for my well being while being sexually aroused at the same time. And I will have to tell you that the strangest part of all of this was that a part of me wanted to sit down next to him. In fact the only thing that kept me from doing just that was that it would have looked odd if I moved my seat with just the two of us on the train. So instead I sat there trying to look casual and hoping my dick wouldn't get so stiff that it would become obvious to this punky guy.

"Fuckin' hot day," he said, his voice low and rough. "Almost nice to be on this train headin' home."

I smiled, nodded my head. "Sure is," I said, knowing that he must be thinking that I'm just some jerk in a suit. I was silent then, reading the advertisements above his head just so I would not look at him and get myself any more horny than I was.

"You like them ads, huh?" he said.

For some reason I felt as if he'd caught me doing something wrong and almost blushed. "Something to do," I said.

"Yeah, not much to do here." He stood up and I could see the outline of his cock in his thin shorts. His prick looked long and thick as it bobbed and swayed back and forth. He scratched his balls and I watched as his shaft moved with his hand. "I like this one here," he said, pointing to some ad that I had to crane my neck around to see. He stood so close to my face that I could almost smell his ball sweat. "Sometimes I think of taking them up on it, you know, going to that trade school and maybe learning a skill."

My neck was getting sore from looking up at where this guy was pointing so I turned around only to see his crotch in front of me. His prick was semi-hard, its massive width and length obvious. That was when the train jerked quickly and the lights began to flicker. The punk lost balance and fell towards me, his crotch falling against my face, the mound of stiffening cock against my lips.

The lights went out as the guy regained his balance. The train came to an abrupt stop, but this time the punk seemed to keep his footing. I could see the punk grabbing his crotch as the lights flickered on.

There was a crackle over the intercom, then the conductor's voice rang out in a muffled garble of words. "There will be a slight delay due to a sudden break in the track. We are sorry for any inconvenience this may cause."

I looked out the window across from me and saw nothing but darkness. "Hope you ain't in a rush," the guy said. "This shit can take forever." He grabbed hold of the overhead bar, leaned back and sighed. The bulge of his stiffening dick swayed back and forth. "I'm not in any rush, but man it sucks being trapped like this."

I wasn't entirely upset, having such a beautiful sight as this man's crotch staring me in the face. I hoped he wouldn't move. He reached down and scratched his balls. "You like that, huh?"

"Like what?" I said, trying to act naive.

"This." He grabbed his crotch so his semi-boner and balls were easy to recognize in his shorts. "I felt your lips on my prick when this train stopped. You like to suck dick? I'm up for it if you are."

At first I said nothing, thinking that perhaps this was some trick and he was about to beat the shit out of me if I agreed. "Come on man, you been looking at it all this time," he said, pulling his thick shaft out of his shorts. "I'm so fucking horny now." He slapped his shaft over my mouth. "You got that nice mouth, too. I just know you can give good head." That was all I needed to hear. I opened my mouth and allowed him to slip the swollen knob between my lips. I sucked on the head, then slowly eased the rest of his shaft down, then out. He kept his hands on the metal bar overhead as my head bobbed on his pole. He sighed and moaned, telling me that he was right, that I was giving him real good head.

His prick was slick with spit when I pulled it out of my mouth. The cock head was ripe and swollen, looking about ready to burst. I reached into his shorts and pulled out his big, hairy nuts and started sucking them. The musty scent of his crotch filled my nostrils, making my cock so hard that it was straining against the inside of my slacks. I was in need of some reciprocation, but wasn't sure this guy would be all too interested in getting me off.

Then he pulled back and his balls popped out of my mouth.

"Come on, man, suck me some more," he said, poking his ripe cock head into my mouth and grabbing my head. He slammed his shaft down my throat and fucked my mouth good and hard. By this time my throat was already accustomed to his prick so I didn't gag too much, just felt his knob ripen even more, getting ready to blow.

He had stamina too. His cock head kept plumping up in my throat as he slammed his meat down my gullet until drool started spilling out of the corners of my mouth. Then he pulled his prick out, gave it a stroke and blew his creamy load against the window behind me. And it was something to watch, the way the first shot of cum leapt from his piss slit and splattered against the glass, then another and another until it seemed like he was spent. Watching his spunk drip down the window, I pulled my prick out of my slacks and started giving it a few strokes.

"No, man," the guy said. He put his hand in his pocket and pulled out a condom. "Not yet, there's still more fuckin' to be done. I want you to fuck my ass."

I looked at him, unable to believe my ears. This little punk wanted me to fuck him up the ass. I would have never imagined that this guy would have ever thought of getting a prick up his butt, but sure enough that was what he wanted. Without saying a word, I grabbed the condom, opened it up and unrolled it over my shaft. The punk was grabbing hold of the overhead railing once more, his shorts bunched down around his ankles. His firm ass cheeks were ready and waiting for my cock. I smoothed my hand over each firm cheek, dipped my middle finger into the hot crack and felt his tight fuck hole with my middle finger. He sighed and spread his legs further apart as I started playing with his pucker. He was waiting for me, for my cock to be shoved up his ass. "You want it?" I said.

"Yeah man, I want it."

I parted his ass cheeks, pressed my cock head against his waiting hole and slowly pushed my shaft inside. His ass was warm and tight. I gradually slid my pole further, listening to him sigh and moan, telling me how good it felt to have my cock up his ass. Once my prick was buried all the way inside his bowels, I reached around and grabbed hold of his dick, which was stiff and still slick with spit. Slowly, I began slipping my shaft out of his fuck hole, feeling his ass ring grip my prick until only the head of my cock was inside him.

"Come on man, don't be a pansy," he said. "Give it to me. Fuck me good and hard."

I slammed my cock up his ass. He pushed his ass against my hips and let out a pleasurable sigh. "Yeah man, just like that. Just like that."

So I did just what he wanted. I grabbed hold of his hips, slid my shaft back until only my cock head was inside, then slammed it up his ass, pulled back and did the same. My hands felt up his sweaty chest as I fucked this guy good and hard. He moaned and sighed, telling me to fuck him harder, to fill him with my cock. I pinched his nipples and he let out a sigh. "Fuck man, that feels good," he moaned. "Give me your hard cock."

Jizm was building up in the head of my cock, eager to be released. I'd held back as much as I could while fucking this guy's ass and didn't know how much longer I could hold out. He was just too damn hot. "I'm going to cum," I said.

"Yeah, give it to me. Give me your fuck juice," he said.

I grabbed hold of his hips and gave his fuck chute a few quick jabs as my cock head began to pulse and spew hot cum. And I swear his ass ring gripped my shaft tighter once I started coming.

Once my balls were empty, I pulled my prick out of his ass and looked at the seat in front of us. There was a pool of jizm on the seat, so I guess he'd been playing with himself as I fucked his ass. He turned towards me and smiled. "You'll need some place to dispose of that," he said, referring to the cum-filled condom that was still gripping my shaft. He looked around and found a discarded paper bag in one corner. I pulled the condom off and tossed it in the bag as the train shuddered, then slowly began to move once more.

We both got dressed as the train clamored on its journey. I watched as the punk used his shirt to clean his spunk off the window and the seat. "I was gonna chuck this thing out anyway," he said.

The train stopped and the doors slid open. "See ya 'round," he said and stepped off the train. A few people boarded the train as I watched him walk down the platform and through the turnstile.

I still see that punk every now and again when riding the train into work, but I have not seen him on my way home from work since. For some reason he doesn't seem quite as dangerous as before. But all in all, he's still hot and I would fuck him on the train again if I had the chance. And believe me, if that can happen to me, it can certainly happen to you.

PARLOR GAMES

I like the feeling of cock in my hand, even if it is my own. Gently running my fingers down the fleshy tube, over the innocuous tubular protrusion that runs along the bottom length and leads to the heart shaped underside of the head, is enough to make me want to blow my load. There is so much pleasure in touching. My partner, Alex, agrees.

When Alex is naked, lying in bed, there is nothing like the sound of his soft breathing, which is like a soothing lullaby. Sometimes, when he's asleep, I like to touch him, feel his wiry pubic hair, the soft fleshy balls, and beneath them, where it's warm and slightly moist. When I get in close I can smell his manly scent, like musk. I like the salty taste of his skin, and the way his nuts roll on my tongue in their loose sack. When I lick his nuts, Alex will stir. I'll feel his hairy leg on my back, hear his soft voice coax me on. Alex will sometimes sit up, run his fingers through my hair as I suck his long, thick shaft. And when he comes, he likes to shoot his load on me, so I can feel it.

I know every inch of Alex's body. Every curve, indentation, and texture has been recorded by my fingertips; his taste, and scent will never be forgotten. I know the pace at which he walks, and the length of his stride. Since Alex has his vision, my perceptions always seem to amaze him.

But this isn't about me, or how a blind man gets laid, this is about how I met Alex.

I met Alex a year ago, at the gym where I work out three times a week. I like to go to the gym during the last few hours before they close; that way there will be fewer people using the equipment. The guy at the front desk, Mark, knows me and always says hello when I walk in. When I first started going to the gym, Mark used to constantly ask if I needed help. Having Mark at my side, giving me advice, making sure I knew where everything was, was like having my own personal trainer. And once I knew how many steps to each of the pieces of equipment, Mark let me alone.

So there I was one day, doing my final bench press, when I sensed someone standing next to me.

"It's only me," Mark said.

Sitting up, I took a breather. "You want to use the bench?" I asked.

"No, just watching. You're doing good."

"Thanks." I brought my elbows back to stretch my pecs, then extended my arms. "I'll be sore as hell in two days."

"It was that good, huh?" Mark rubbed my shoulder.

I heard the clank of weights falling, then a soft groan a few feet away. "I'm closing up soon."

There was the pad of rubber against floor as someone stepped away from the Nautilus machines.

"I'm done for the day anyhow," I said. "Want me to skip the shower so you can get out?"

"No, not at all. I've got a lot of paperwork to get done, so take your time. I just wanted to see how you were doing, is all."

"Are you sure?" I asked.

"Hey, I'm sure. It's just you and Alex back there, I'm not too concerned." Then I heard Mark's heavy steps as he walked back to the front desk.

Grabbing the towel at my feet, I wiped sweat off my brow. I'd worked out hard, and my t-shirt was soaked with sweat. What I needed was a good hot shower. So I went to the men's locker room, sat on the long wooden bench that ran between two rows of metal lockers, took off my sneakers and socks. I sensed someone else a few feet down from me, then remembered Mark telling me that Alex would be changing up, too. Alex was still breathing heavy, so I guessed he'd worked himself pretty hard. I pulled off my shirt, then threw it in the locker.

"How was your workout?" I asked.

"Man, it was tough," Alex said. "Sometimes I overdo it, you know. I'm still kind of new at this, only been working out for a few months."

"You'll learn," I said, hearing Alex's bare feet hit the floor as he walked up behind me. I stood up and put my thumbs in the elastic band of my shorts, then felt Alex's thick fingers on my back. I stopped. He kissed my neck, then slid his hands down and around my waist. Alex's big, thick hands felt good on my body. He rubbed my stomach, then pressed his thumbs against my nipples. I didn't move, or even try to continue to undress.

"It's okay," Alex whispered, his voice low and soft. "We're

alone."

It was obvious we were alone, but I didn't say a thing. Alex had made my dick spring to life, and I wasn't about to stop him. Instead I leaned back, feeling his fingers dip into the waistband of my shorts. He pulled my shorts down to my knees. And as he pulled, his tongue slid down my spine, then licked the crack of my ass. I leaned forward and pressed my hands against the cold metal of the lockers as he separated my ass cheeks and rubbed his thumbs against my hole. He slapped my ass, then stood up.

"You're so fucking hot," he said. "I had to get you alone."

I couldn't believe this guy had just felt me up and now wanted to talk. I touched his chest, which had thick, coarse hairs on the tops of his developed pectorals, but nothing on his firm stomach. His thick cock was fully erect, and had to be a good seven inches, with a plump head. I stroked his shaft a few times, then he stepped away.

With long, even strides, he walked around the bench until he was standing in front of me. I reached out and touched his chest, rubbed my thumbs over the delicate flesh of his aureoles, then the firm nipples. My fingers caressed the smooth skin of his stomach, then went up to the patch of coarse hair on his upper chest. Then I slid my hands lower, feeling how his torso became more narrow towards his waist.

"You like that?" he asked in a hushed voice.

"Yes," I said, then kissed his navel. His skin was salty with sweat. I played with his heavy, low hanging balls, and took in the scent of his manhood. It wasn't long before I felt the blunted head of his cock rubbing against my chin. Running my fingers along the length of the massive rod, I felt a thin, serpentine vein bulge out from beneath the skin. The heart-like head was ripe, and seemed eager to throb at my touch.

"Shit, that feels good," he said.

Reaching behind him, I felt his smooth, firm ass. The curve was so delicate, and the crack between the two mounds was damp. I slid my fingers inside the crack, spread his ass cheeks, then moved my fingertips down to his puckered hole.

"You like that?" I asked.

"Yes," he moaned. "Finger my hole, man."

Rubbing my face against his thick dick, I pushed the tips of my fingers into his tight hole. He moaned, and I rubbed my face against his shaft, feeling the head plump up even more. Precum oozed out of the piss slit and dampened my cheek. Then I pushed my fingers further inside him. "Oh fuck," he called out, "I'm going to cum." Then his cock head pulsed, and spewed hot jizm on my cheek and neck.

Reaching down, he grabbed under my arms and brought me into a standing position. His warm, moist tongue licked every last drop of his spunk off my body.

"I want to see you get off," he said, the scent of cum fresh on his breath. He spit into his hand, then grabbed hold of my prick and gave it a long, slow stroke. "How does this feel?"

"Good," I said, feeling my knees give way to the pleasure in my groin. I held onto his firm torso, licked his sweaty neck. Alex's big, thick hands slowly stroked up the length of my shaft, right up and over the delicate head, then back down in steady repetitions. It didn't take long before I felt the pressure in my cock head build to the point where I could no longer hold back. My toes curled, and I tightened my grip on Alex's body. I let out a groan, then heard the first cum shot hit the thin metal locker in front of me. Then I shot again, and again, until the last few drops of jizm were squeezed out of my knob.

Once I finished coming and had regained my composure, I took a seat on the bench. "What I really need now is a shower."

"You and me both," Alex said. "Let me tell you, you're fucking hot."

"So are you." I reached out and rubbed his smooth cheek, feeling a flush of heat from his face.

"Oh man, you don't know that," Alex said.

"Yes, I do." I pulled my hand away from Alex's face, and fought the urge to slap him. "You're just too young to know it."

"And how old do you think I am?" Alex's voice echoed against the tiled room.

"Young enough to forgive."

"And how old is that?"

I closed the padlock on my locker door. "Early twenties."

"I'm twenty-four," Alex said. "That's not exactly early twenties."

"Then what is it?"

"Mid twenties." There was the soft thump of a towel hitting the lockers. "So, you want to hook up again?"

"Sure," I said. "Remind me to give you a business card before I leave."

Surprisingly enough, Alex did call. We hooked up for a couple of hot sessions at my place, and I got to know the sound of his step, and the feel of his body. The first time he dropped by he seemed surprised that I knew where everything was in my apartment, which was not a cool thing to say. If I didn't like fucking his ass so much, I would have told him to leave and not come back. By our third meeting, everything seemed to be going well between us. Alex's no-brain comments were fewer, and I was actually beginning to enjoy having him around for brief encounters. Then one day he dropped by unannounced.

One day I answered the front door, and the person on the other side handed me a piece of paper. I gently ran my fingers over the raised letters and read the message: I won't say a word, you tell me who I am. The note was insulting, and my first instinct was to slam the door closed, but then I had a feeling it was Alex and sex was imminent.

I did not smell any cologne from the man who pushed past me, but did know the heavy footfalls, and the dull thud of rubber against hardwood floors. It was Alex. The cushions on the sofa squealed, then there was the dull thud of one sneaker hitting the floor. Walking up to him, I reached out and ran my fingers through his soft, short hair. I decided to tell him off after we fucked.

"A parlor game," I said, then calmly walked to the overstuffed chair to the left of the sofa by four steps. Pressing my fingertips together, I looked across the room. "Well then, if I'm going to guess who you are, you'll have to do a few things for me. I'll need you to take off your clothes, then go into my bedroom and get the lubricant and a condom."

I heard Alex pulling off his clothes, the soft sound of jeans being pulled down, and sneakers being pushed under the coffee table. Then there was the sound of his walk as he made his way into the bedroom. That was when I undressed, then sat down once more. I gave my shaft a playful stroke, getting it even more erect than it already was.

Alex stepped back into the room. His breathing was heavy, and I knew he was standing directly in front of me. I looked off to my left, away from him. "Put the condom on my cock, then I want you to lube it up and sit on it."

Alex unrolled the latex over my prick, then I felt his firm grip on my dick as he lubed it up. Grabbing hold of the back of the chair, Alex placed each leg over the arm rests, and lowered himself down on my shaft. His pucker gripped my prick, slowly easing it into his warm fuck chute. I brought my hands beneath his ass, feeling the firm rounded mounds. When he had my entire rod buried deep inside him, he eased back up. Pushing his ass up, I helped him along.

"You feel good," I sighed. Cum was already rising up my shaft, building pressure at the head. Alex's cock head rubbed precum onto my chest as he slowly rode my shaft. His breath slapped my face in quick, hot bursts.

"You feel so good, Alex," I said.

"Man, I knew you'd figured me out," Alex said. "You're amazing."

At that time I cared more about pumping my hot load up Alex's hole than being amazing. And it was about to shoot, and soon. "Play with yourself," I said.

"I need my hands for leverage," Alex said.

"Hold onto me."

Alex gripped my shoulders as I stood, took four steps to the right, then gently lowered us onto the floor. Lying on my back, Alex continued to ride my prick, only much faster, and with greater force. His ass was so damn hot and warm and tight, and his sphincter gripped my cock with a fury all its own.

"Jerk yourself off," I said, feeling myself on the brink of orgasm.

"Shit, man, I'm going to cum," Alex said, then I felt the first shot of hot spunk hit my chest, and that was when my body shuddered and I blew huge gobs of jizm.

By the time Alex had finished coming, my chest was covered with his fuck juice. I peeled off the condom, then walked to the bathroom. Alex was behind me the whole time. I tossed the rubber in the trash, then felt Alex's hands wrap around my waist and pull me close to him.

"You drive me fucking wild," Alex said.

"Well, wild man, I need to take a shower," I said. "You're welcome to join me." I turned on the shower, then waited for the water to get hot.

"I like a hot shower," Alex said.

"I take it you're joining me."

"Sure am," Alex said, then let out a nervous chuckle. "Don't drop the soap."

I fought the urge to roll my eyes. "And if I do, I'll pick it up."

"Hey, man, it's an expression," Alex said as I peeled back the shower curtain.

And he was right, it was an expression. I breathed in and tasted the steam billowing out of the shower. It had to be too hot. It was, so I turned up the cold, then asked Alex if he wanted to go in first. He did, then let out a howl.

"Still too hot?" I asked.

"No, it's fine."

I stepped into the shower. Hot spray hit Alex's body, and misted my face.

"You're sensitive about it, sometimes," Alex said.

"About what?" I asked.

"You know."

"My eyesight? No, not really," I said. "It's just a little annoying when people think it's more than it is."

"It's a part of you," Alex said.

For once, Alex had said the right thing. Instead of telling him that, I wrapped my arms around his waist, my fingers reaching down to the suds surrounding his cock and balls. Alex leaned his head back, and I pressed my lips against his wet flesh. His dick became hard in my hand, and I gave it a gentle stroke.

"Man, you keep that up and we'll have to do it again," Alex said.

That was my intent.

BOOKS FROM LEYLAND PUBLICATIONS / G.S PRESS

AIDS RISK REDUCTION GUIDELINES
FOR HEALTHIER SEX

As given by Bay Area Physicians for Human Rights

NO RISK: *Most of these activities involve only skin-to-skin contact, thereby avoiding exposure to blood, semen, and vaginal secretions. This assumes there are no breaks in the skin.* 1) Social kissing (dry). 2) Body massage, hugging. 3) Body to body rubbing (frottage). 4) Light S&M (without bruising or bleeding). 5) Using one's own sex toys. 6) Mutual masturbation (male or external female). Care should be taken to avoid exposing the partners to ejaculate or vaginal secretions. Seminal, vaginal and salivary fluids should not be used as lubricants.

LOW RISK: *In these activities small amounts of certain body fluids might be exchanged, or the protective barrier might break causing some risk.* 1) Anal or vaginal intercourse with condom. Studies have shown that HIV does not penetrate the condom in simulated intercourse. Risk is incurred if the condom breaks or if semen spills into the rectum or vagina. The risk is further reduced if one withdraws before climax. 2) Fellatio interruptus (sucking, stopping before climax). Pre-ejaculate fluid may contain HIV. Saliva or other natural protective barriers in the mouth may inactivate virus in pre-ejaculate fluid. Saliva may contain HIV in low concentration. The insertive partner should warn the receptive partner before climax to prevent exposure to a large volume of semen. If mouth or genital sores are present, risk is increased. Likewise, action which causes mouth or genital injury will increase risk. 3) Fellatio with condom (sucking with condom) Since HIV cannot penetrate an intact condom, risk in this practice is very low unless breakage occurs. 4) Mouth-to-mouth kissing (French kissing, wet kissing) Studies have shown that HIV is present in saliva in such low concentration that salivary exchange is unlikely to transmit the virus. Risk is increased if sores in the mouth or bleeding gums are present. 5) Oral-vaginal or oral-anal contact with protective barrier. e.g. a latex dam, obtainable through a local dental supply house, may be used. Do not reuse latex barrier, because sides of the barrier may be reversed inadvertently. 6) Manual anal contact with glove (manual anal or (fisting) or manual vaginal (internal) contact with glove. If the glove does not break, virus transmission should not occur. However, significant trauma can still be inflicted on the rectal tissues leading to other medical problems, such as hemorrhage or bowel perforation. 7) Manual vaginal contact with glove (internal). See above.

MODERATE RISK: *These activities involve tissue trauma and/or exchange of body fluids which may transmit HIV or other sexually transmitted disease.* 1) Fellatio (sucking to climax). Semen may contain high concentrations of HIV and if absorbed through open sores in the mouth or digestive tract could pose risk. 2) Oral-anal contact (rimming). HIV may be contained in blood-contaminated feces or in the anal rectal lining. This practice also poses high risk of transmission of parasites and other gastrointestinal infections. 3) Cunnilingus (oral-vaginal contact). Vaginal secretions and menstrual blood have been shown to harbor HIV, thereby causing risk to the oral partner if open lesions are present in the mouth or digestive tract. 4) Manual rectal contact (fisting). Studies have indicated a direct association between fisting and HIV infection for both partners. This association may be due to concurrent use of recreational drugs, bleeding, pre-fisting semen exposure, or anal intercourse with ejaculation. 5) Sharing sex toys. 6) Ingestion of urine. HIV has not been shown to be transmitted via urine; however, other immunosuppressive agents or infections may be transmitted in this manner.

HIGH RISK: *These activities have been shown to transmit HIV.* 1) Receptive anal intercourse without condom. All studies imply that this activity carries the highest risk of transmitting HIV. The rectal lining is thinner than that of the vagina or the mouth thereby permitting ready absorption of the virus from semen or pre-ejaculate fluid to the blood stream. One laboratory study suggests that the virus may enter by direct contact with rectal lining cells without any bleeding. 2) Insertive anal intercourse without condom. Studies suggest that men who participate only in this activity are at less risk of being infected than their partners who are rectally receptive; however the risk is still significant. It carries high risk of infection by sexually transmitted diseases. 3) Vaginal intercourse without condom.